LOVE
in
BLACK
and
WHITE

LOVE
in
BLACK
and
WHITE

Robert James Waller

SINCLAIR-STEVENSON

First published in Great Britain by
Sinclair-Stevenson Limited
7/8 Kendrick Mews
London SW7 3HG England

Copyright © 1992 by Robert James Waller

First published in 1992 in the United States of America by Warner Books, Inc.
under the title The Bridges of Madison County

British Library Cataloguing in Publication Data
A CIP catalogue record for this book is available from the British Library.

ISBN: 1 85619 154 0

Filmset in Baskerville by
Selwood Systems, Midsomer Norton
Printed and bound in Great Britain by
Butler & Tanner Ltd, Frome and London

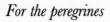

For the peregrines

Author's Note

THERE ARE SONGS that come free from the blue-eyed grass, from the dust of a thousand country roads. This is one of them. In late afternoon, in the autumn of 1989, I'm at my desk, looking at a blinking cursor on the computer screen before me, and the telephone rings.

On the other end of the wire is a former Iowan named Michael Johnson. He lives in Florida now. A friend from Iowa has sent him one of my books. Michael Johnson has read it; his sister, Carolyn, has read it; and they have a story in which they think I might be interested. He is circumspect, refusing to say anything about the story, except that he and Carolyn are willing to travel to Iowa to talk with me about it.

That they are prepared to make such an effort intrigues me, in spite of my scepticism about such offers. So I agree to meet with them in Des Moines the following week. At a Holiday Inn near the airport, the introductions are made, awkwardness gradually declines, and the two of them sit across from me, evening coming down outside, light snow falling.

They extract a promise: If I decide not to write the story, I must agree never to disclose what transpired in Madison County, Iowa, in 1965 or other related events that followed over the next twenty-four years. All right, that's reasonable. After all, it's their story, not mine.

So I listen. I listen hard, and I ask hard questions. And they talk. On and on they talk. Carolyn cries openly at times, Michael struggles not to. They show me documents and magazine clippings and a set of journals written by their mother, Francesca.

Room service comes and goes. Extra coffee is ordered. As they talk, I begin to see the images. First you must have the images, then come the words. And I begin to hear the words, begin to see them on pages of writing. Some time just after midnight, I agree to write the story—or at least attempt it.

Their decision to make this information public was a difficult one for them. The circumstances are delicate, involving their mother and, more tangentially, their father. Michael and Carolyn recognized that coming forth with the story might result in tawdry gossip and unkind debasement of whatever memories people have of Richard and Francesca Johnson.

Yet in a world where personal commitment in all of its forms seems to be shattering and love has become a matter of convenience, they both felt this remarkable tale was worth the telling. I believed then, and I believe even more strongly now, they were correct in their assessment.

In the course of my research and writing, I asked to meet with Michael and Carolyn three more times. On each occasion, and without complaint, they travelled to Iowa. Such was their eagerness to make sure the story was told accurately. Sometimes we merely talked; sometimes we slowly drove the roads of Madison County while they pointed out places having a significant role in the story.

In addition to the help provided by Michael and Carolyn, the story as I tell it here is based on information contained in the journals of Francesca Johnson; research conducted in the northwestern United States, particularly Seattle and Bellingham, Washington; research carried out quietly in Madison County, Iowa; information gleaned from the photographic essays of Robert Kincaid; assistance provided by magazine editors; detail supplied by manufacturers of photographic films and equipment; and long discussions with several wonderful elderly people in the county home at Barnesville, Ohio, who remembered Kincaid from his boyhood days.

In spite of the investigative effort, gaps remain. I have added a little of my own imagination in those instances, but only when I could make reasoned judgments flowing from the intimate familiarity with Francesca Johnson and Robert Kincaid I gained through my research. I am confident that I have come very close to what actually happened.

One major gap involves the exact details of a trip made across the northern United States by Kincaid. We knew he made this journey, based on a number of photographs that subsequently were published, a brief mention of it by Francesca Johnson in her journals, and handwritten notes he left with a magazine editor. Using these sources as my guide, I retraced what I believe was the path he took from Bellingham to Madison County in August of 1965. Driving toward Madison County at the end of my travels, I felt I had, in many ways, become Robert Kincaid.

Still, attempting to capture the essence of Kincaid was the most challenging part of my research and writing. He is an elusive figure. At times he seems rather ordinary. At other times ethereal, perhaps even spectral. In his work he was a consummate professional. Yet he saw himself as a peculiar kind of male animal becoming obsolete in a world given over to increasing amounts of organization. He once talked about the 'merciless wail' of time in his head, and Francesca Johnson characterized him as living 'in strange, haunted places, far back along the stems of Darwin's logic.'

Two other intriguing questions are still unanswered. First, we have been unable to determine what became of Kincaid's photographic files. Given the nature of his work, there must have been thousands, probably hundreds of thousands, of photographs. These never have been recovered. Our best guess—and this would be consistent with the way he saw himself and his place in the world—is that he destroyed them prior to his death.

The second question deals with his life from 1975 to 1982. Very little information is available. We know he earned a sparse living as a portrait photographer in Seattle for several years and continued to photograph the Puget Sound area. Other than that, we have nothing. One interesting note is that all letters mailed to him by the Social Security Administration and Veterans Administration were marked 'Return to Sender' in his handwriting and sent back.

Preparing and writing this book has altered my world view, transformed the way I think, and, most of all, reduced my level of cynicism about what is possible in the arena of human relationships. Coming to know Francesca Johnson and Robert Kincaid as I have through my research, I find the boundaries of such relationships can be extended farther than I previously thought. Perhaps you will have the same experience in reading this story.

That will not be easy. In an increasingly callous world, we all exist with our own carapaces of scabbed-over sensibilities. Where great passion leaves off and mawkishness begins, I'm not sure. But our tendency to scoff at the possibility of the former and to label genuine and profound feelings as maudlin makes it difficult to enter the realm of gentleness required to understand the story of Francesca Johnson and Robert Kincaid. I know I had to overcome that tendency initially before I could begin writing.

If, however, you approach what follows with a willing suspension of disbelief, as Coleridge put it, I am confident you will experience what I have experienced. In the indifferent spaces of your heart, you may even find, as Francesca Johnson did, room to dance again.

ROBERT JAMES WALLER
Cedar Falls, Iowa
Summer 1991

Robert Kincaid

ON THE MORNING of August 8, 1965, Robert Kincaid locked the door to his small two-room apartment on the third floor of a rambling house in Bellingham, Washington. He carried a knapsack full of photography equipment and a suitcase down wooden stairs and through a hallway to the back, where his old Chevrolet pickup truck was parked in a space reserved for residents of the building.

Another knapsack, a medium-size ice chest, two tripods, cartons of Camel cigarettes, a Thermos, and a bag of fruit were already inside. In the truck box was a guitar case. Kincaid arranged the knapsacks on the seat and put the cooler and tripods on the floor. He climbed into the truck box and wedged the guitar case and suitcase into a corner of the box, bracing them with a spare tyre lying on its side and securing both cases to the tyre with a length of clothesline rope. Under the worn spare he shoved a black tarpaulin.

He stepped in behind the wheel, lit a Camel, and went through his mental checklist: two hundred rolls of assorted film, mostly slow-speed Kodachrome; tripods; cooler; three cameras and five lenses; jeans and khaki slacks; shirts; wearing photo vest. Okay. Anything else he could buy on the road if he had forgotten it.

Kincaid wore faded Levi's, well-used Red Wing field boots, a khaki shirt, and orange suspenders. On his wide leather belt was fastened a Swiss Army knife in its own case.

He looked at his watch: eight-seventeen. The truck started on the second try, and he backed out, shifted gears, and moved slowly down the alley under hazy sun. Through the streets of Bellingham he went, heading south on Washington 11, running along the coast of Puget Sound for a few miles, then following the highway as it swung east a little before meeting U.S. Route 20.

Turning into the sun, he began the long, winding drive through the Cascades. He liked this country and felt unpressed, stopping now and then to make notes about interesting possibilities for future expeditions or to shoot what he called 'memory snapshots.' The purpose of these cursory photographs was to remind him of places he might want to visit again and approach more seriously. In late afternoon he turned north at Spokane, picking up U.S. Route 2, which would take him halfway across the northern United States to Duluth, Minnesota.

He wished for the thousandth time in his life that he

had a dog, a golden retriever, maybe, for travels like this and to keep him company at home. But he was frequently away, overseas much of the time, and it would not be fair to the animal. Still, he thought about it anyway. In a few years he would be getting too old for the hard fieldwork. 'I might get a dog then,' he said to the coniferous green rolling by his truck window.

Drives like this always put him into a taking-stock mood. The dog was part of it. Robert Kincaid was as alone as it's possible to be—an only child, parents both dead, distant relatives who had lost track of him and he of them, no close friends.

He knew the names of the man who owned the corner market in Bellingham and the proprietor of the photographic store where he bought his supplies. He also had formal, professional relationships with several magazine editors. Other than that, he knew scarcely anyone well, nor they him. Gypsies make difficult friends for ordinary people, and he was something of a gypsy.

He thought about Marian. She had left him nine years ago after five years of marriage. He was fifty-two now; that would make her just under forty. Marian had dreams of becoming a musician, a folksinger. She knew all of the Weavers' songs and sang them pretty well in the coffeehouses of Seattle. When he was home in the old days, he drove her to gigs and sat in the audience while she sang.

His long absences—two or three months some-times—were hard on the marriage. He knew that. She was aware of what he did when they decided to get married, and each of them had a vague sense that it could all be handled somehow. It couldn't. When he came home from photographing a story in Iceland, she was gone. The note read: 'Robert, it didn't work out. I left you the Harmony guitar. Stay in touch.'

He didn't stay in touch. Neither did she. He signed the divorce papers when they arrived a year later and caught a plane for Australia the next day. She had asked for nothing except her freedom.

At Kalispell, Montana, he stopped for the night, late. The Cozy Inn looked inexpensive, and was. He carried his gear into a room containing two table lamps, one of which had a burned-out bulb. Lying in bed, reading *The Green Hills of Africa* and drinking a beer, he could smell the paper mills of Kalispell. In the morning he jogged for forty minutes, did fifty push-ups, and used his cameras as small hand weights to complete the routine.

Across the top of Montana he drove, into North Dakota and the spare, flat country he found as fas-cinating as the mountains or the sea. There was a kind of austere beauty to this place, and he stopped several times, set up a tripod, and shot some black-and-whites of old farm buildings. This landscape appealed to his minimalist leanings. The Indian reservations were depressing, for all of the reasons everybody knows and ignores. Those kinds of settlements were no better in northwestern Washington, though, or anywhere else he had seen them.

On the morning of August 14, two hours out of Duluth, he sliced northeast and took a back road up to Hibbing and the iron mines. Red dust floated in the air, and there were big machines and trains specially designed to haul the ore to freighters at Two Harbors on Lake Superior. He spent an afternoon looking around Hibbing and found it not to his liking, even if Bob Zimmerman-Dylan was from there originally.

The only song of Dylan's he had ever really cared for was 'Girl from the North Country.' He could play and sing that one, and he hummed the words to himself as he left behind the place with giant red holes in the earth. Marian had shown him some chords and how to handle basic arpeggios to accompany himself. 'She left me with more than I left her,' he said once to a boozy riverboat pilot in a place called McElroy's Bar, somewhere in the Amazon basin. And it was true.

The Superior National Forest was nice, real nice. Voyageur country. When he was young, he'd wished the old voyageur days were not over so he could become one. He drove by meadows, saw three moose, a red fox, and lots of deer. At a pond he stopped and shot some reflections on the water made by an odd-shaped tree branch. When he finished he sat on the running board of his truck, drinking coffee, smoking a Camel, and listening to the wind in the birch trees.

'It would be good to have someone, a woman,' he thought, watching the smoke from his cigarette blow out over the pond. 'Getting older puts you in that frame of mind.' But with him gone so much, it would be tough on the one left at home. He'd already learned that.

When he was home in Bellingham, he occasionally dated the creative director for a Seattle advertising agency. He had met her while doing a corporate job. She was forty-two, bright, and a nice person, but he didn't love her, would never love her.

Sometimes they both got a little lonely, though, and would spend an evening together, going to a movie, having a few beers, and making pretty decent love later on. She'd been around—two marriages, worked as a waitress in several bars while attending college. Invariably, after they'd completed their lovemaking and were lying together, she'd tell him, 'You're the best, Robert, no competition, nobody even close.'

He supposed that was a good thing for a man to hear, but he was not all that experienced and had no way of knowing whether or not she was telling the truth anyway. But she did say something one time that haunted him: 'Robert, there's a creature inside of you that I'm not good enough to bring out, not strong enough to reach. I sometimes have the feeling you've been here a long time, more than one lifetime, and that you've dwelt in private places none of the rest of us has even dreamed about. You frighten me, even though you're gentle with me. If I didn't fight to control myself with you, I feel like I might lose my centre and never get back.'

He knew in an obscure way what she was talking about. But he couldn't get his hands on it himself. He'd had these drifting kinds of thoughts, a wistful sense of the tragic combined with intense physical and intellectual power, even as a young boy growing up in a small Ohio town. When other kids were singing 'Row, Row, Row Your Boat,' he was learning the melody and English words to a French cabaret song.

He liked words and images. 'Blue' was one of his favourite words. He liked the feeling it made on his lips and tongue when he said it. Words have physical feeling, not just meaning, he remembered thinking when he was young. He liked other words, such as 'distant,' 'woodsmoke,' 'highway,' 'ancient,' 'passage,' 'voyageur,' and 'India' for how they sounded, how they tasted, and what they conjured up in his mind. He kept lists of words he liked posted in his room.

Then he joined the words into phrases and posted those as well:

> *Too close to the fire*
>
> *I came from the East with a small band of travellers*

*The constant chirping of those who would
save me and those who would sell me.*

*Talisman, Talisman, show me your secrets.
Helmsman, Helmsman, turn me for home.*

Lying naked where blue whales swim.

*She wished him steaming trains that left from
winter stations.*

*Before I became a man, I was an arrow—
long time ago.*

Then there were the places whose names he liked:
the Somali Current, the Big Hatchet Mountains, the
Malacca Strait, and a long list of others. The sheets of
paper with words and phrases and places eventually
covered the walls of his room.

Even his mother noticed something different about
him. He never spoke a word until he was three, then
began talking in complete sentences, and he could read
extremely well by five. In school he was an indifferent
student, frustrating the teachers.

They looked at his IQ scores and talked to him
about achievement, about doing what he was capable of
doing, that he could become anything he wanted to
become. One of his high school teachers wrote the
following in an evaluation of him: 'He believes that
"IQ tests are a poor way to judge people's abilities,
failing as they do to account for magic, which has its

own importance, both by itself and as a complement to logic." I suggest a conference with his parents.'

His mother met with several teachers. When the teachers talked about Robert's quietly recalcitrant behaviour in light of his abilities, she said, 'Robert lives in a world of his own making. I know he's my son, but I sometimes have the feeling that he came not from my husband and me, but from another place to which he's trying to return. I appreciate your interest in him, and I'll try once more to encourage him to do better in school.'

But he had been content to read all the adventure and travel books in the local library and kept to himself otherwise, spending days along the river that ran through the edge of town, ignoring proms and football games and other things that bored him. He fished and swam and walked and lay in long grass listening to distant voices he fancied only he could hear. 'There are wizards out there,' he used to say to himself. 'If you're quiet and open enough to hear them, they're out there.' And he wished he had a dog to share these moments.

There was no money for college. And no desire for it, either. His father worked hard and was good to his mother and him, but the job in a valve factory didn't leave much for other things, including the care of a dog. He was eighteen when his father died, so with the Great Depression bearing down hard, he enlisted in the army as a way of supporting his mother and himself. He stayed there four years, but those four years changed his life.

In the mysterious way that military minds work, he was assigned to a job as photographer's assistant, though he had no idea of even how to load a camera. But in that work, he discovered his profession. The technical details were easy for him. Within a month he was not only doing the darkroom work for two of the staff photographers, but also was allowed to shoot simple projects himself.

One of the photographers, Jim Peterson, liked him and spent extra time showing him the subtleties of photography. Robert Kincaid checked out photo books and art books from the Fort Monmouth town library and studied them. Early on, he particularly liked the French impressionists and Rembrandt's use of light.

Eventually he began to see that light was what he photographed, not objects. The objects merely were the vehicles for reflecting the light. If the light was good, you could always find something to photograph. The 35-millimetre camera was beginning to emerge then, and he purchased a used Leica at a local camera store. He took it down to Cape May, New Jersey, and spent a week of his leave there photographing life along the shore.

Another time he rode a bus to Maine and hitch-hiked up the coast, caught the dawn mail boat out to Isle Au Haut from Stonington, and camped, then took a ferry across the Bay of Fundy to Nova Scotia. He began keeping notes of his camera settings and places he wanted to visit again. When he came out of the army at twenty-two, he was a pretty decent shooter and found work in New York assisting a well-known fashion photographer.

The female models were beautiful; he dated a few and fell partially in love with one before she moved to Paris and they drifted apart. She had said to him: 'Robert, I don't know who or what you are for sure, but please come visit me in Paris.' He told her he would, meant it when he said it, but never got there. Years later when he was doing a story on the beaches of Normandy, he found her name in the Paris book, called, and they had coffee at an outdoor cafe. She was married to a cinema director and had three children.

He couldn't get very keen on the idea of fashion. People threw away perfectly good clothes or hastily had them made over according to the instructions of European fashion dictators. It seemed dumb to him, and he felt lessened doing the photography. 'You are what you produce,' he said as he left this work.

His mother died during his second year in New York. He went back to Ohio, buried her, and sat before a lawyer, listening to the reading of the will. There wasn't much. He didn't expect there would be anything. But he was surprised to find his parents had accumulated a little equity in the tiny house on Franklin Street where they had lived all their married lives. He sold the house and bought first-class equipment with the money. As he paid the camera salesman, he thought of the years his father had worked for those dollars and the plain life his parents had led.

Some of his work began to appear in small magazines. Then *National Geographic* called. They had seen a calendar shot he had taken out on Cape May. He talked with them, got a minor assignment, executed it professionally, and was on his way.

The military asked him back in 1943. He went with the Marines and slogged his way up South Pacific beaches, cameras swinging from his shoulders, lying on his back, photographing the men coming off amphibious landing craft. He saw the terror on their faces, felt it himself. Saw them cut in two by machine-gun fire, saw them plead to God and their mothers for help. He got it all, survived, and never became hooked on the so-called glory and romance of war photography.

Coming out of the service in 1945, he called *National Geographic*. They were ready for him, anytime. He bought a motorcycle in San Francisco, ran it south to Big Sur, made love on a beach with a cellist from Carmel, and turned north to explore Washington. He liked it there and decided to make it his base.

Now, at fifty-two, he was still watching the light. He had been to most of the places posted on his boyhood walls and marvelled he actually was there when he visited them, sitting in the Raffles Bar, riding up the Amazon on a chugging riverboat, and rocking on a camel through the Rajasthani desert.

The Lake Superior shore was as nice as he'd heard it was. He marked down several locations for future reference, took some shots to jog his memory later on, and headed south along the Mississippi River toward Iowa. He'd never been to Iowa but was taken with the hills of the northeast part along the big river. Stopping in the little town of Clayton, he stayed at a fisherman's motel and spent two mornings shooting the towboats and an afternoon on a tug at the invitation of a pilot he met in a local bar.

Cutting over to U.S. Route 65, he went through Des Moines early on a Monday morning, August 16, 1965, swung west at Iowa 92, and headed for Madison County and the covered bridges that were supposed to be there, according to *National Geographic*. They were there all right; the man in the Texaco station said so and gave him directions, just fairish directions, to all seven.

The first six were easy to find as he mapped out his strategy for photographing them. The seventh, a place called Roseman Bridge, eluded him. It was hot, he was hot, Harry—his truck—was hot, and he was wandering around on gravel roads that seemed to lead nowhere except to the next gravel road.

In foreign countries, his rule of thumb was, 'Ask three times.' He had discovered that three responses, even if they were all wrong, gradually vectored you in to where you wanted to go. Maybe twice would be enough here.

A mailbox was coming up, sitting at the end of a lane about one hundred yards long. The name on the box read 'Richard Johnson, RR 2.' He slowed down and turned up the lane, looking for guidance.

When he pulled into the yard, a woman was sitting on the front porch. It looked cool there, and she was drinking something that looked even cooler. She came off the porch toward him. He stepped from the truck and looked at her, looked closer, and then closer still. She was lovely, or had been at one time, or could be again. And immediately he began to feel the old clumsiness he always suffered around women to whom he was even faintly attracted.

Francesca

DEEP AUTUMN WAS birthday time for Francesca, and cold rain swept against her frame house in the south Iowa countryside. She watched the rain, looked through it toward the hills along Middle River, thinking of Richard. He had died on a day like this, eight years ago, from something with a name she would rather not remember. But Francesca thought of him now and his sturdy kindness, his steady ways, and the even life he had given her.

The children had called. Neither of them could make it home again this year for her birthday, though it was her sixty-seventh. She understood, as she always did. Always had. Always would. They were both in mid-career, running hard, managing a hospital, teaching students, Michael getting into his second marriage, Carolyn struggling with her first. Secretly she was glad they never seemed to arrange a visit on her birthday; she had her own ceremonies reserved for that day.

This morning her friends from Winterset had stopped by with a birthday cake. Francesca made coffee, while the talk ran to grandchildren and the town, to Thanksgiving and what to get for Christmas for whom. The quiet laughter and the rise and fall of conversation from the living room were comforting in their familiarity and reminded Francesca of one small reason why she had stayed here after Richard's death.

Michael had touted Florida, Carolyn New England. But she had remained in the hills of south Iowa, on the land, keeping her old address for a special reason, and she was glad she had done that.

Francesca had watched them leave at lunchtime. They drove their Buicks and Fords down the lane, turned onto the paved county road, and headed toward Winterset, wiper blades pushing aside the rain. They were good friends, though they would never understand what lay inside of her, would not understand even if she told them.

Her husband had said she would find good friends, when he brought her here after the war, from Naples. He said, 'Iowans have their faults, but one of them is not lack of caring.' And that was true, is true.

She had been twenty-five when they met—out of the university for three years, teaching at a private school for girls, wondering about her life. Most of the young Italian men were dead or injured or in POW camps or broken by the fighting. Her affair with Niccolo, a professor of art at the university, who painted all day and took her on wild, reckless tours of the underside of

Naples at night, had been over for a year, done in finally by the unceasing disapproval of her traditional parents.

She wore ribbons in her black hair and clung to her dreams. But no handsome sailors disembarked looking for her, no voices came up to her window from the streets below. The hard press of reality brought her to the recognition that her choices were constrained. Richard offered a reasonable alternative: kindness and the sweet promise of America.

She had studied him in his soldier's uniform as they sat in a cafe in the Mediterranean sunlight, saw him looking earnestly at her in his midwestern way, and came to Iowa with him. Came to have his children, to watch Michael play football on cold October nights, to take Carolyn to Des Moines for her prom dresses. She exchanged letters with her sister in Naples several times each year and had returned there twice, when each of her parents had died. But Madison County was home now, and she had no longing to go back again.

The rain stopped in midafternoon, then resumed its ways just before evening. In the twilight, Francesca poured a small glass of brandy and opened the bottom drawer of Richard's rolltop desk, the walnut piece that had passed down through three generations of his family. She took out a manila envelope and brushed her hand across it slowly, as she did each year on this day.

The postmark read 'Seattle, WA, Sep 12 '65.' She

always looked at the postmark first. That was part of the ritual. Then to the address written in longhand: 'Francesca Johnson, RR 2, Winterset, Iowa.' Next the return address, carelessly scrabbled in the upper left: 'Box 642, Bellingham, Washington.' She sat in a chair by the window, looked at the addresses, and concentrated, for contained in them was the movement of his hands, and she wanted to bring back the feel of those hands on her twenty-two years ago.

When she could feel his hands touching her, she opened the envelope, carefully removed three letters, a short manuscript, two photographs, and a complete issue of *National Geographic* along with clippings from other issues of the magazine. There, in grey light fading, she sipped her brandy, looking over the rim of her glass to the handwritten note clipped on the typed manuscript pages. The letter was on his stationery, simple stationery that said only 'Robert Kincaid, Writer-Photographer' at the top in discreet lettering.

September 10, 1965

Dear Francesca,

Enclosed are two photographs. One is the shot I took of you in the pasture at sunrise. I hope you like it as much as I do. The other is of Roseman Bridge before I removed your note tacked to it.

I sit here trolling the grey areas of my mind for every detail,

*every moment, of our time together. I ask myself over and over,
'What happened to me in Madison County, Iowa?' And I struggle
to bring it together. That's why I wrote the little piece, 'Falling
from Dimension Z,' I have enclosed, as a way of trying to sift
through my confusion.*

*I look down the barrel of a lens, and you're at the end of it. I
begin work on an article, and I'm writing about you. I'm not
even sure how I got back here from Iowa. Somehow the old truck
brought me home, yet I barely remember the miles going by.*

*A few weeks ago, I felt self-contained, reasonably content.
Maybe not profoundly happy, maybe a little lonely, but at least
content. All of that has changed.*

*It's clear to me now that I have been moving toward you and
you toward me for a long time. Though neither of us was aware
of the other before we met, there was a kind of mindless certainty
humming blithely along beneath our ignorance that ensured we
would come together. Like two solitary birds flying the great
prairies by celestial reckoning, all of these years and lifetimes we
have been moving toward one another.*

*The road is a strange place. Shuffling along, I looked up and
you were there walking across the grass toward my truck on an
August day. In retrospect, it seems inevitable—it could not have
been any other way—a case of what I call the high probability
of the improbable.*

*So here I am walking around with another person inside of
me. Though I think I put it better the day we parted when I said
there is a third person we have created from the two of us. And I
am stalked now by that other entity.*

Somehow, we must see each other again. Any place, anytime.

Call me if you ever need anything or simply want to see me.

I'll be there, pronto. Let me know if you can come out here sometime—anytime. I can arrange plane fare, if that's a problem. I'm off to southeast India next week, but I'll be back in late October.

I Love You,
Robert

P. S., The photo project in Madison County turned out fine. Look for it in NG next year. Or tell me if you want me to send a copy of the issue when it's published.

Francesca Johnson set her brandy glass on the wide oak windowsill and stared at an eight-by-ten black-and-white photograph of herself. Sometimes it was hard for her to remember how she had looked then, twenty-two years ago. In tight faded jeans, sandals, and a white T-shirt, her hair blowing in the morning wind as she leaned against a fence post.

Through the rain, from her place by the window, she could see the post where the old fence still circumscribed the pasture. When she rented out the land, after Richard died, she stipulated the pasture must be kept intact, left untouched, even though it was empty now and had turned to meadow grass. The first serious lines were just beginning to show on her face in the photograph. His camera had found them. Still, she was pleased with what she saw. Her hair was black, and her body was full and warm, filling out the jeans just about right. Yet it was her face at which she stared. It was the face of a woman desperately in love with the man taking the picture.

She could see him clearly also, down the flow of her memory. Each year she ran all of the images through her mind, meticulously, remembering everything, forgetting nothing, imprinting all of it, forever, like tribesmen passing down an oral history through the generations. He was tall and thin and hard, and he moved like the grass itself, without effort, gracefully. His silver-grey hair hung well below his ears and nearly always looked dishevelled, as if he had just come in from a long sea voyage through a stiff wind and had tried to brush it into place with his hands.

His narrow face, high cheekbones, and hair falling over his forehead set off light blue eyes that seemed never to stop looking for the next photograph. He had smiled at her, saying how fine and warm she looked in early light, asked her to lean against the post, and then moved around her in a wide arc, shooting from knee level, then standing, then lying on his back with the camera pointed up at her.

She had been slightly embarrassed at the amount of film he used but pleased by the amount of attention he paid to her. She hoped none of the neighbours were out early on their tractors. Though on that particular morning she hadn't cared too much about neighbours and what they thought.

He shot, loaded film, changed lenses, changed

cameras, shot some more, and talked quietly to her as he worked, always telling her how good she looked to him and how much he loved her. 'Francesca, you're incredibly beautiful.' Sometimes he stopped and just stared at her, through her, around her, inside of her.

Her nipples were clearly outlined where they pressed against the cotton T-shirt. She had been strangely unconcerned about that, about being naked under the shirt. More, she was glad of it and was warmed knowing that he could see her breasts so clearly down his lenses. Never would she have dressed this way around Richard. He would not have approved. Indeed, before meeting Robert Kincaid, she would not have dressed this way anytime.

Robert had asked her to arch her back ever so slightly, and he had whispered then, 'Yes, yes, that's it, stay there.' That was when he had taken the photograph at which she now stared. The light was perfect, that's what he had said—'cloudy bright' was his name for it— and the shutter clicked steadily as he moved around her.

He was lithe; that was the word she had thought of while watching him. At fifty-two his body was all lean muscle, muscle that moved with the kind of intensity and power that comes only to men who work hard and take care of themselves. He told her he had been a combat photographer in the Pacific, and Francesca could imagine him coming up smoke-drenched beaches with the marines, cameras banging against him, one to his eye, the shutter almost on fire with the speed of his picture taking.

She looked at the picture again, studied it. I did look good, she thought, smiling to herself at the mild self-admiration. 'I never looked that good before or after. It was him.' And she took another sip of brandy while the rain climbed up and rode hard on the back of November wind.

Robert Kincaid was a magician of sorts, who lived within himself in strange, almost threatening places. Francesca had sensed as much immediately on a hot, dry Monday in August 1965, when he stepped out of his truck onto her driveway. Richard and the children were at the Illinois State Fair, exhibiting the prize steer that received more attention than she did, and she had the week to herself.

She had been sitting on the front porch swing, drinking iced tea, casually watching the dust spiral up from under a pickup coming down the county road. The truck was moving slowly, as if the driver were looking for something, stopped just short of her lane, then turned up it toward the house. Oh, God, she had thought. Who's this?

She was barefoot, wearing jeans and a faded blue workshirt with the sleeves rolled up, shirttail out. Her long black hair was fastened up by a tortoiseshell comb her father had given her when she left the old country.

41

The truck rolled up the lane and stopped near the gate to the wire fence surrounding the house.

Francesca stepped off the porch and walked unhurriedly through the grass toward the gate. And out of the pickup came Robert Kincaid, looking like some vision from a never-written book called *An Illustrated History of Shamans*.

His tan military-style shirt was tacked down to his back with perspiration; there were wide, dark circles of it under his arms. The top three buttons were undone, and she could see tight chest muscles just below the plain silver chain around his neck. Over his shoulders were wide orange suspenders, the kind worn by people who spent a lot of time in wilderness areas.

He smiled. 'I'm sorry to bother you, but I'm looking for a covered bridge out this way, and I can't find it. I think I'm temporarily lost.' He wiped his forehead with a blue bandanna and smiled again.

His eyes looked directly at her, and she felt something jump inside. The eyes, the voice, the face, the silver hair, the easy way he moved his body, old ways, disturbing ways, ways that draw you in. Ways that whisper to you in the final moment before sleep comes, when the barriers have fallen. Ways that rearrange the molecular space between male and female, regardless of species.

The generations must roll, and the ways whisper only of that single requirement, nothing more. The power is infinite, the design supremely elegant. The ways are unswerving, their goal is clear. The ways are simple; we have made them seem complicated. Francesca sensed this without knowing she was sensing it, sensed it at the level of her cells. And there began the thing that would change her forever.

A car went past on the road, trailing dust behind it, and honked. Francesca waved back at Floyd Clark's brown arm sticking out of his Chevy and turned back to the stranger. 'You're pretty close. The bridge is only about two miles from here.' Then, after twenty years of living the close life, a life of circumscribed behaviour and hidden feelings demanded by a rural culture, Francesca Johnson surprised herself by saying, 'I'll be glad to show it to you, if you want.'

Why she did that, she never had been sure. A young girl's feelings rising like a bubble through water and bursting out, maybe, after all these years. She was not shy, but not forward, either. The only thing she could ever conclude was that Robert Kincaid had drawn her in somehow, after only a few seconds of looking at him.

He was obviously taken aback, slightly, by her offer. But he recovered quickly and with a serious look on his face said he'd appreciate that. From the back steps she picked up the cowboy boots she wore for farm chores and walked out to his truck, following him around to the passenger side.

'Just take me a minute to make room for you; lots of gear 'n' stuff in here.' He mumbled mostly to himself

43

as he worked, and she could tell he was a little flustered, and a little shy about the whole affair.

He was rearranging canvas bags and tripods, a Thermos bottle and paper sacks. In the back of the pickup were an old tan Samsonite suitcase and a guitar case, both dusty and battered, both tied to a spare tyre with a piece of clothesline rope.

The door of the truck swung shut, banging him in the rear as he mumbled and sorted and stuffed paper coffee cups and banana peels into a brown grocery bag that he tossed into the truck box when he was finished. Finally he removed a blue-and-white ice chest and put that in the back as well. In faded red paint on the green truck door was printed 'Kincaid Photography, Bellingham, Washington.'

'Okay, I think you can squeeze in there now.' He held the door, closed it behind her, then went around to the driver's side and with a peculiar, animal-like grace stepped in behind the wheel. He looked at her, just a quick glance, smiled slightly, and said, 'Which way?'

'Right.' She motioned with her hand. He turned the key, and the out-of-tune engine ground to a start. Along the lane toward the road, bouncing, his long legs working the pedals automatically, old Levi's running down over leather-laced, brown field boots that had seen lots of foot miles go by.

He leaned over and reached into the glove compartment, his forearm accidentally brushing across her lower thigh. Looking half out the windshield and half into the compartment, he took out a business card and handed it to her. 'Robert Kincaid, Writer-Photographer.' His address was printed there, along with a phone number.

'I'm out here on assignment for *National Geographic*,' he said. 'You familiar with the magazine?'

'Yes.' Francesca nodded, thinking, Isn't everybody?

'They're doing a piece on covered bridges, and Madison County, Iowa, apparently has some interesting ones. I've located six of them, but I guess there's at least one more, and it's supposed to be out in this direction.'

'It's called Roseman Bridge,' said Francesca over the noise of the wind and tyres and engine. Her voice sounded strange, as if it belonged to someone else, to a teenage girl leaning out of a window in Naples, looking far down city streets toward the trains or out at the harbour and thinking of distant lovers yet to come. As she spoke, she watched the muscles in his forearm flex when he shifted gears.

Two knapsacks were beside her. The flap of one was closed, but the other was folded back, and she could see the silver-coloured top and black back of a camera sticking out. The end of a film box, 'Kodachrome II, 25. 36 Exposures,' was taped to the camera back. Stuffed behind the packs was a tan vest with many pockets. Out of one pocket dangled a thin cord with a plunger on the end.

Behind her feet were two tripods. They were badly scratched, but she could read part of the worn label on one: 'Gitzo.' When he had opened the glove box, she noticed it was crammed with notebooks, maps, pens, empty film canisters, loose change, and a carton of Camel cigarettes.

'Turn right at the next corner,' she said. That gave her an excuse to glance at the profile of Robert Kincaid. His skin was tanned and smooth and shiny with sweat. He had nice lips; for some reason she had noticed that right away. And his nose was like that she had seen on Indian men during a vacation the family had taken out west when the children were young.

He wasn't handsome, not in any conventional sense. Nor was he homely. Those words didn't seem to apply to him. But there was something, something about him. Something very old, something slightly battered by the years, not in his appearance, but in his eyes.

On his left wrist was a complicated-looking watch with a brown, sweat-stained leather band. A silver bracelet with some intricate scrollwork clung to his right wrist. It needed a good rubbing with silver polish, she thought, then chastised herself for being caught up in the trivia of small-town life she had silently rebelled against through the years.

Robert Kincaid pulled a pack of cigarettes from his shirt pocket, shook one halfway out, and offered it to her. For the second time in five minutes, she surprised herself and took the cigarette. What am I doing? she thought. She had smoked years ago but gave it up under the steady thump of criticism from Richard. He shook out another one, put it between his lips, and flicked a gold Zippo lighter into flame, holding it toward her while he kept his eyes on the road.

She cupped her hands around the lighter to hold the wind in abeyance and touched his hand to steady it against the bouncing of the truck. It took only an instant for her to light the cigarette, but that was long enough to feel the warmth of his hand and the tiny hairs along the back of it. She leaned back and he swung the lighter toward his own cigarette, expertly forming his wind cup, taking his hands off the steering wheel for no more than a second.

Francesca Johnson, farmer's wife, rested against the dusty truck seat, smoked the cigarette, and pointed. 'There it is, just around the curve.' The old bridge, peeling red in colour, tilting slightly from all the years, sat across a small stream.

Robert Kincaid had smiled then. He quickly looked at her and said, 'It's great. A sunrise shot.' He stopped a hundred feet from the bridge and got out, taking the open knapsack with him. 'I'm going to do a little reconnaissance for a few minutes, do you mind?' She shook her head and smiled back.

Francesca watched him walk up the country road, taking a camera from the knapsack and then slinging the bag over his left shoulder. He had done that thousands of times, that exact movement. She could tell by the fluidity of it. As he walked, his head never stopped moving, looking from side to side, then at the bridge, then at the trees behind the bridge. Once he turned and looked back at her, his face serious.

In contrast with the local folks, who fed on gravy and potatoes and red meat, three times a day for some of them, Robert Kincaid looked as if he ate nothing but fruit and nuts and vegetables. Hard, she thought. He looks hard, physically. She noticed how small his rear was in his tight jeans—she could see the outlines of his billfold in the left pocket and the bandanna in the right one—and how he seemed to move over the ground with unwasted motion.

It was quiet. A redwing blackbird sat on fence wire and looked in at her. A meadowlark called from the roadside grass. Nothing else moved in the white sun of August.

Just short of the bridge, Robert Kincaid stopped. He stood there for a moment, then squatted down, looking through the camera. He walked to the other side of the road and did the same thing. Then he moved into the cover of the bridge and studied the beams and floor planks, looked at the stream below through a hole in the side.

Francesca snuffed out her cigarette in the ashtray, swung open the door, and put her boots on the gravel.

She glanced around to make sure none of her neighbours' cars were coming and walked toward the bridge. The sun was a hammer in late afternoon, and it looked cooler inside the bridge. She could see his silhouette at the other end until he disappeared down the incline toward the stream.

Inside, she could hear pigeons burbling softly in their nests under the eves and put the palm of her hand on the side planking, feeling the warmth. Graffiti was scrawled on some of the planks: 'Jimbo—Denison, Iowa.' 'Sherry + Dubby.' 'Go Hawks!' The pigeons kept on burbling softly.

Francesca peeked through a crack between two of the side planks, down toward the stream where Robert Kincaid had gone. He was standing on a rock in the middle of the little river, looking toward the bridge, and she was startled to see him wave. He jumped back to the bank and moved easily up the steep grade. She kept watching the water until she sensed his boots on the bridge flooring.

'It's real nice, real pretty here,' he said, his voice reverberating inside the covered bridge.

Francesca nodded. 'Yes, it is. We take these old bridges for granted around here and don't think much about them.'

He walked to her and held out a small bouquet of wildflowers, black-eyed Susans. 'Thanks for the guided tour.' He smiled softly. 'I'll come back at dawn one of these days and get my shots.' She felt something inside of her again. Flowers. Nobody gave her flowers, even on special occasions.

'I don't know your name,' he said. She realized then that she had not told him and felt dumb about that. When she did, he nodded and said, 'I caught the smallest trace of an accent. Italian?'

'Yes. A long time ago.'

The green truck again. Along the gravel roads with the sun lowering itself. Twice they met cars, but it was nobody Francesca knew. In the four minutes it took to reach the farm, she drifted, feeling unravelled and strange. More of Robert Kincaid, writer-photographer, that's what she wanted. She wanted to know more and clutched the flowers on her lap, held them straight up, like a schoolgirl coming back from an outing.

The blood was in her face. She could feel it. She hadn't done anything or said anything, but she felt as if she had. The truck radio, indistinguishable almost in the roar of road and wind, carried a steel guitar song, followed by the five o'clock news.

He turned the truck up the lane. 'Richard is your husband?' He had seen the mailbox.

'Yes,' said Francesca, slightly short of breath. Once her words started, they kept on coming. 'It's pretty hot. Would you like an ice tea?'

He looked over at her. 'If it's all right, I sure would.'

'It's all right,' she said.

She directed him—casually, she hoped—to park the pickup around behind the house. What she didn't need was for Richard to come home and have one of the neighbour men say, 'Hey, Dick, havin' some work done at the place; saw a green pickup there last week. Knew Frannie was home so I did'n bother to check on it.'

Up broken cement steps to the back porch door. He held the door for her, carrying his camera knapsacks. 'Awful hot to leave the equipment in the truck,' he had said when he pulled them out.

A little cooler in the kitchen, but still hot. The collie snuffled around Kincaid's boots, then went out on the back porch and flopped down while Francesca removed ice from metal trays and poured sun tea from a half-gallon glass jug. She knew he was watching her as he sat at the kitchen table, long legs stretched in front of him, brushing his hair with both hands.

'Lemon?'

'Yes, please.'

'Sugar?'

'No, thanks.'

The lemon juice dribbled slowly down the side of a glass, and he saw that, too. Robert Kincaid missed little.

Francesca set the glass before him. Put her own on the other side of the Formica-topped table and her bouquet in water, in an old jelly glass with renderings of Donald Duck on it. Leaning against the counter, she balanced on one leg, bent over, and took off a boot.

51

Stood on her bare foot and reversed the process for the other boot.

He took a small drink of tea and watched her. She was about five feet six, fortyish or a little older, pretty face, and a fine, warm body. But there were pretty women everywhere he travelled. Such physical matters were nice, yet, to him, intelligence and passion born of living, the ability to move and be moved by subtleties of the mind and spirit, were what really counted. That's why he found most young women unattractive, regardless of their exterior beauty. They had not lived long enough or hard enough to possess those qualities that interested him.

But there was something in Francesca Johnson that did interest him. There was intelligence; he could sense that. And there was passion, though he couldn't quite grasp what that passion was directed toward or if it was directed at all.

Later, he would tell her that in ways undefinable, watching her take off her boots that day was one of the most sensual moments he could remember. Why was not important. That was not the way he approached his life. 'Analysis destroys wholes. Some things, magic things, are meant to stay whole. If you look at their pieces, they go away.' That's what he had said.

She sat at the table, one leg curled under her, and pulled back strands of hair that had fallen over her face, refastening them with the tortoiseshell comb. Then, remembering, she rose and went to the end cupboard, took down an ashtray, and set it on the table where he could reach it.

With that tacit permission, he pulled out a pack of Camels and held it toward her. She took one and noticed it was slightly wet from his heavy perspiring. Same routine. He held the gold Zippo, she touched his hand to steady it, felt his skin with her fingertips, and sat back. The cigarette tasted wonderful, and she smiled.

'What is it you do, exactly—I mean with the photography?'

He looked at his cigarette and spoke quietly. 'I'm a contract shooter—uh, photographer—for *National Geographic*, part of the time. I get ideas, sell them to the magazine, and do the shoot. Or they have something they want done and contact me. Not a lot of room for artistic expression; it's a pretty conservative publication. But the pay is decent. Not great, but decent, and steady. The rest of the time I write and photograph on my own hook and send pieces to other magazines. If things get tough, I do corporate work, though I find that awfully confining.

'Sometimes I write poetry, just for myself. Now and then I try to write a little fiction, but I don't seem to have a feeling for it. I live north of Seattle and work around that area quite a bit. I like shooting the fishing boats and Indian settlements and landscapes.

'The *Geographic* work often keeps me at a location for a

couple of months, particularly for a major piece on something like part of the Amazon or the North African desert. Ordinarily I fly to an assignment like this and rent a car. But I felt like driving through some places and scouting them out for future reference. I came down along Lake Superior, I'll go back through the Black Hills. How about you?'

Francesca hadn't expected him to ask. She stammered for a moment. 'Oh, gosh, nothing like you do. I got my degree in comparative literature. Winterset was having trouble finding teachers when I arrived here in 1946, and the fact that I was married to a local man who was a veteran made me acceptable. So I picked up a teaching certificate and taught high school English for a few years. But Richard didn't like the idea of me working. He said he could support us, and there was no need for it, particularly when our two children were growing. So I stopped and became a farm wife full-time. That's it.'

She noticed his iced tea was almost gone and poured him some more from the jug.

'Thanks. How do you like it here in Iowa?'

There was a moment of truth in this. She knew it. The standard reply was, 'Just fine. It's quiet. The people are real nice.'

She didn't answer immediately. 'Could I have another cigarette?' Again the pack of Camels, again the lighter, again touching his hand, lightly. Sunlight

54

walked across the back porch floor and onto the dog, who got up and moved out of sight. Francesca, for the first time, looked into the eyes of Robert Kincaid.

'I'm supposed to say, "Just fine. It's quiet. The people are real nice." All of that's true, mostly. It is quiet. And the people *are* nice, in certain ways. We all help each other out. If someone gets sick or hurt, the neighbours pitch in and pick corn or harvest oats or do whatever needs to be done. In town, you can leave your car unlocked and let your children run without worrying about them. There are a lot of good things about the people here, and I respect them for those qualities.

'But'—she hesitated, smoked, looked across the table at Robert Kincaid—'it's not what I dreamed about as a girl.' The confession, at last. The words had been there for years, and she had never said them. She had said them now to a man with a green pickup truck from Bellingham, Washington.

He said nothing for a moment. Then: 'I scribbled something in my notebook the other day for future use, just had the idea while driving along; that happens a lot. It goes like this: "The old dreams were good dreams; they didn't work out, but I'm glad I had them." I'm not sure what that means, but I'll use it somewhere. So I think I kind of know how you feel.'

Francesca smiled at him then. For the first time, she smiled warm and deep. And the gambler's instincts took over. 'Would you like to stay for supper? My family's away, so I don't have too much on hand, but I can figure out something.'

'Well, I get pretty tired of grocery stores and restaurants. That's for sure. So if it's not too much bother, I'd like that.'

'You like pork chops? I could fix that with some vegetables from the garden.'

'Just the vegetables would be fine for me. I don't eat meat. Haven't for years. No big deal, I just feel better that way.'

Francesca smiled again. 'Around here that point of view would not be popular. Richard and his friends would say you're trying to destroy their livelihood. I don't eat much meat myself; I'm not sure why, I just don't care for it. But every time I try a meatless supper on the family, there are howls of rebellion. So I've pretty much given up trying. It'll be fun figuring out something different for a change.'

'Okay, but don't go to a lot of trouble on my account. Listen, I've got a bunch of film in my cooler. I need to dump out the melted ice water and organize things a bit. It'll take me a little while.' He stood up and drank the last of his tea.

She watched him go through the kitchen doorway, across the porch, and into the yard. He didn't let the screen door bang like everyone else did but instead shut it gently. Just before he went out, he squatted down to pet the collie, who acknowledged the attention with several sloppy licks along his arms.

Upstairs, Francesca ran a quick bath and, while drying off, peered over the top of the cafe curtain toward the farmyard. His suitcase was open, and he was washing himself, using the old hand pump. She should have told him he could shower in the house if he wanted. She had meant to, balked for a moment at the level of familiarity that implied to her, and then, floating around in her own confusion, forgot to say anything.

But Robert Kincaid had washed up under worse conditions. Out of buckets of rancid water in tiger country, out of his canteen in the desert. In her farmyard, he had stripped to the waist and was using his dirty shirt as a combination washcloth and towel. 'A towel,' she scolded herself. 'At least a towel; I could have done that for him.'

His razor caught the sunlight, where it lay on cement beside the pump, and she watched him soap his face and shave. He was—There's the word again, she thought—hard. He wasn't bigbodied, a little over six feet, a little toward thin. But he had large shoulder muscles for his size, and his belly was flat as a knife blade. He didn't look however old he was, and he didn't look like the local men with too much gravy over biscuits in the morning.

During the last shopping trip to Des Moines, she had bought new perfume—Wind Song—and she used it now, sparingly. What to put on? It didn't seem right for her to dress up too much, since he was still in his working clothes. Long-sleeved white shirt, sleeves rolled to just below the elbows, a clean pair of jeans, sandals. The gold hoop earrings Richard said made her look like a hussy and a gold bracelet. Hair pulled back with a clip, hanging down her back. That felt right.

When she came into the kitchen, he was sitting there with his knapsacks and cooler, wearing a clean khaki shirt, with the orange suspenders running over it. On the table were three cameras and five lenses, and a fresh package of Camels. The cameras all said 'Nikon' on them. So did the black lenses, short ones and middling ones and a longer one. The equipment was scratched, dented in places. But he handled it carefully, yet casually, wiping and brushing and blowing.

He looked up at her, serious face again, shy face. 'I have some beer in the cooler. Like one?'

'Yes, that would be nice.'

He took out two bottles of Budweiser. When he lifted the lid, she could see clear plastic boxes with film stacked like cordwood in them. There were four more bottles of beer besides the two he removed.

Francesca slid open a drawer to look for an opener. But he said, 'I've got it.' He took the Swiss Army knife from its case on his belt and flicked out the bottle opener on it, using it expertly.

He handed her a bottle and raised his in a half salute:

'To covered bridges in the late afternoon or, better yet, on warm, red mornings.' He grinned.

Francesca said nothing but smiled softly and raised her bottle a little, hesitantly, awkwardly. A strange stranger, flowers, perfume, beer, and a toast on a hot Monday in late summer. It was almost more than she could deal with.

'There was somebody a long time ago who was thirsty on an August afternoon. Whoever it was studied their thirst, rigged up some stuff, and invented beer. That's where it came from, and a problem was solved.' He was working on a camera, almost talking to it as he tightened a screw on its top with a jeweller's screwdriver.

'I'm going out to the garden for a minute. I'll be right back.'

He looked up. 'Need help?'

She shook her head and walked past him, feeling his eyes on her hips, wondering if he watched her all the way across the porch, guessing that he did.

She was right. He watched her. Shook his head and looked again. Watched her body, thought of the intelligence he knew she possessed, wondered about the other things he sensed in her. He was drawn to her, fighting it back.

The garden was in shade now. Francesca moved through it with a dishpan done in cracked white enamel. She gathered carrots and parsley, some parsnips and onions and turnips.

When she entered the kitchen, Robert Kincaid was repacking the knapsacks, neatly and precisely, she noticed. Everything obviously had its place and always was placed in its place. He had finished his beer and opened two more, even though she was not quite done with hers. She tilted back her head and finished the first one, handing him the empty bottle.

'Can I do something?' he asked.

'You can bring in the watermelon from the porch and a few potatoes from the bucket out there.'

He moved so easily that she was amazed at how quickly he went to the porch and returned, melon under his arm, four potatoes in his hands. 'Enough?'

She nodded, thinking how ghostlike he seemed. He set them on the counter beside the sink where she was cleaning the garden vegetables and returned to his chair, lighting a Camel as he sat down.

'How long will you be here?' she asked, looking down at the vegetables she was working on.

'I'm not sure. This is a slow time for me, and my deadline for the bridge pictures is still three weeks away. As long as it takes to get it right, I guess. Probably about a week.'

'Where are you staying? In town?'

'Yes. A little place with cabins. Something-or-other Motor Court. I just checked in this morning. Haven't even unloaded my gear yet.'

'That's the only place to stay, except for Mrs

Carlson's; she takes in roomers. The restaurants will be a disappointment, though, particularly for someone with your eating habits.'

'I know. It's an old story. But I've learned to make do. This time of year it's not so bad; I can find fresh produce in the stores and at stands along the road. Bread and a few other things, and I make it work, approximately. It's nice to be invited out like this, though. I appreciate it.'

She reached along the counter and flipped on a small radio, one with only two dials and tan cloth covering the speakers. 'With time in my pocket, and the weather on my side ...' a voice sang, guitars chunking along underneath. She kept the volume low.

'I'm pretty good at chopping vegetables,' he offered.

'Okay, there's the cutting board, a knife's in the drawer right below it. I'm going to fix a stew, so kind of cube the vegetables.'

He stood two feet from her, looking down, cutting and chopping the carrots and turnips, parsnips and onions. Francesca peeled potatoes into the sink, aware of being so close to a strange man. She had never thought of peeling potatoes as having little slanting feelings connected with it.

'You play the guitar? I saw the case in your truck.'

'A little bit. It keeps me company, not too much more than that. My wife was an early folkie, way before the music became popular, and she got me going on it.'

Francesca had stiffened slightly at the word *wife*. Why, she didn't know. He had a right to be married, but somehow it didn't fit him. She didn't want him to be married.

'She couldn't stand the long shoots when I'd be gone for months. I don't blame her. She pulled out nine years ago. Divorced me a year later. We never had children, so it wasn't complicated. Took one guitar, left the el cheapo with me.'

'You hear from her?'

'No, never.'

That was all he said. Francesca didn't push it. But she felt better, selfishly, and wondered again why she should care one way or the other.

'I've been to Italy, twice,' he said. 'Where you from, originally?'

'Naples.'

'Never made it there. I was in the north once, doing some shooting along the River Po. Then again for a piece on Sicily.'

Francesca peeled potatoes, thinking of Italy for a moment, conscious of Robert Kincaid beside her.

Clouds had moved up in the west, splitting the sun into rays that splayed in several directions. He looked out the window above the sink and said, 'God light. Calendar companies love it. So do religious magazines.'

'Your work sounds interesting,' Francesca said. She felt a need to keep neutral conversation going.

'It is. I like it a lot. I like the road, and I like making pictures.'

She noticed he'd said 'making' pictures. 'You make pictures, not take them?'

'Yes. At least that's how I think of it. That's the difference between Sunday snapshooters and someone who does it for a living. When I'm finished with that bridge we saw today, it won't look quite like you expect. I'll have made it into something of my own, by lens choice, or camera angle, or general composition, and most likely by some combination of all of those.

'I don't just take things as given; I try to make them into something that reflects my personal consciousness, my spirit. I try to find the poetry in the image. The magazine has its own style and demands, and I don't always agree with the editor's taste; in fact, most of the time I don't. And that bothers them, even though they decide what goes in and what gets left out. I guess they know their readership, but I wish they'd take a few more chances now and then. I tell them that, and it bothers them.

'That's the problem in earning a living through an art form. You're always dealing with markets, and markets—mass markets—are designed to suit average tastes. That's where the numbers are. That's the reality, I guess. But, as I said, it can become pretty confining. They let me keep the shots they don't use, so at least I have my own private files of stuff I like.

'And, once in a while, another magazine will take one or two, or I can write an article on a place I've been and illustrate it with something a little more daring than *National Geographic* prefers.

'Sometime I'm going to do an essay called "The Virtues of Amateurism" for all of those people who wish they earned their living in the arts. The market kills more artistic passion than anything else. It's a world of safety out there, for most people. They want safety, the magazines and manufacturers give them safety, give them homogeneity, give them the familiar and comfortable, don't challenge them.

'Profit and subscriptions and the rest of that stuff dominate art. We're all getting lashed to the great wheel of uniformity.

'The marketing people are always talking about something called "consumers." I have this image of a fat little man in baggy Bermuda shorts, a Hawaiian shirt, and a straw hat with beer-can openers dangling from it, clutching fistfuls of dollars.'

Francesca laughed quietly, thinking about safety and comfort.

'But I'm not complaining too much. Like I said, the travelling is good, and I like fooling with cameras and being out of doors. The reality is not exactly what the song started out to be, but it's not a bad song.'

Francesca supposed that, for Robert Kincaid, this

was everyday talk. For her, it was the stuff of literature. People in Madison County didn't talk this way, about these things. The talk was about weather and farm prices and new babies and funerals and government programmes and athletic teams. Not about art and dreams. Not about realities that kept the music silent, the dreams in a box.

He finished chopping vegetables. 'Anything else I can do?'

She shook her head. 'No, it's about under control.'

He sat at the table again, smoking, taking a drink of beer now and then. She cooked, sipping on her beer between tasks. She could feel the alcohol, even this small amount of it. On New Year's Eve, at the Legion Hall, she and Richard would have some drinks. Other than that, not much, and there seldom was liquor in the house, except for a bottle of brandy she had bought once in some vague spasm of hope for romance in their country lives. The bottle was still unopened.

Vegetable oil, one and one-half cups of vegetables. Cook until light brown. Add flour and mix well. Add water, a pint of it. Add remaining vegetables and seasonings. Cook slowly, about forty minutes.

With the cooking under way, Francesca sat across from him once again. Modest intimacy descended upon the kitchen. It came, somehow, from the cooking. Fixing supper for a stranger, with him chopping turnips and, therefore, distance, beside you, removed some of the strangeness. And with the loss of strangeness, there was space for intimacy.

He pushed the cigarettes toward her, the lighter on top of the package. She shook one out, fumbled with the lighter, felt clumsy. It wouldn't catch. He smiled a little, carefully took the lighter from her hand, and flipped the flint wheel twice before it caught. He held it, she lit her cigarette. Around men she usually felt graceful in comparison to them. Not around Robert Kincaid, though.

A white sun had turned big red and lay just over the cornfields. Through the kitchen window she could see a hawk riding the early evening updraughts. The seven o'clock news and market summary were on the radio. And Francesca looked across the yellow Formica toward Robert Kincaid, who had come a long way to her kitchen. A long way, across more than miles.

'It already smells good,' he said, pointing toward the stove. 'It smells . . . quiet.' He looked at her.

'Quiet? Could something smell quiet?' She was thinking about the phrase, asking herself. He was right. After the pork chops and steaks and roasts she cooked for the family, this was quiet cooking. No violence involved anywhere down the food chain, except maybe for pulling up the vegetables. The stew cooked quietly and smelled quiet. It was quiet here in the kitchen.

'If you don't mind, tell me a little about your life in

Italy.' He was stretched out on the chair, his right leg crossed over his left at the ankles.

Silence bothered her around him, so she talked. Told him about her growing years, the private school, the nuns, her parents—housewife, bank manager. About standing along the sea wall as a teenager and watching ships from all over the world. About the American soldiers that came later. About meeting Richard in a cafe where she and some girlfriends were drinking coffee. The war had disrupted lives, and they wondered if they would ever get married. She was silent about Niccolo.

He listened, saying nothing, nodding in under-standing occasionally. When she finally paused, he said, 'And you have children, did you say?'

'Yes. Michael is seventeen. Carolyn is sixteen. They both go to school in Winterset. They're in 4-H; that's why they're at the Illinois State Fair. Showing Carolyn's steer.

'Something I've never been able to adapt to, to understand, is how they can lavish such love and care on the animals and then see them sold for slaughter. I don't dare say anything about it, though. Richard and his friends would be down on me in a flash. But there's some kind of cold, unfeeling contradiction in that busi-ness.'

She felt guilty mentioning Richard's name. She hadn't done anything, anything at all. Yet she could feel guilt, a guilt born of distant possibilities. And she wondered how to manage the end of the evening and if she had got herself into something she couldn't handle. Maybe Robert Kincaid would just leave. He seemed pretty quiet, nice enough, even a little bashful.

As they talked on, the evening turned blue, light fog brushing the meadow grass. He opened two more beers for them while Francesca's stew cooked, quietly. She rose and dropped dumplings into boiling water, turned, and leaned against the sink, feeling warm toward Robert Kincaid from Bellingham, Washington. Hoping he wouldn't leave too early.

He ate two helpings of the stew with quiet good manners and told her twice how fine it was. The watermelon was perfect. The beer was cold. The evening was blue. Francesca Johnson was forty-five years old, and Hank Snow sang a train song on KMA, Shenandoah, Iowa.

Ancient Evenings,
Distant Music

Now what? thought Francesca. Supper over, sitting there.

He took care of it. 'How about a walk out in the meadow? It's cooling down a little.' When she said yes, he reached into a knapsack and pulled out a camera, draping the strap over his shoulder.

Kincaid pushed open the back porch door and held it for her, followed her out, then shut it gently. They went down the cracked sidewalk, across the gravelled farmyard, and onto the grass east of the machine shed. The shed smelled like warm grease.

When they came to the fence, she held down the barbed wire with one hand and stepped over it, feeling the dew on her feet around the thin sandal straps. He executed the same manoeuvre, easily swinging his boots over the wire.

'Do you call this a meadow or a pasture?' he asked.

'Pasture, I guess. The cattle keep the grass short. Watch out for their leavings.' A moon nearly full was coming up the eastern sky, which had turned azure with the sun just under the horizon. On the road below, a car rocketed past, loud muffler. The Clark boy. Quarterback on the Winterset team. Dated Judy Leverenson.

It had been a long time since she had taken a walk like this. After supper, which was always at five, there was the television news, then the evening programmes, watched by Richard and sometimes by the children when they had finished their homework. Francesca usually read in the kitchen—books from the Winterset library and the book club she belonged to, history and poetry and fiction—or sat on the front porch in good weather. The television bored her.

When Richard would call, 'Frannie, you've got to see this!' she'd go in and sit with him for a while. Elvis always generated such a summons. So did the Beatles when they first appeared on *The Ed Sullivan Show*. Richard looked at their hair and kept shaking his head in disbelief and disapproval.

For a short time, red streaks cut across part of the sky. 'I call that "bounce,"' Robert Kincaid said, pointing upward. 'Most people put their cameras away too soon. After the sun goes down, there's often a period of really nice light and colour in the sky, just for a few minutes, when the sun is below the horizon but bounces its light off the sky.'

Francesca said nothing, wondering about a man to whom the difference between a pasture and a meadow seemed important, who got excited about sky colour, who wrote a little poetry but not much fiction. Who played the guitar, who earned his living by images and carried his tools in knapsacks. Who seemed like the wind. And moved like it. Came from it, perhaps.

He looked upward, hands in his Levi's pockets, camera hanging against his left hip. 'The silver apples of the moon/The golden apples of the sun.' His mid-range baritone said the words like that of a professional actor.

She looked over at him. 'W.B. Yeats, "The Song of Wandering Ængus."'

'Right. Good stuff, Yeats. Realism, economy, sensuousness, beauty, magic. Appeals to my Irish heritage.'

He had said it all, right there in five words. Francesca had laboured to explain Yeats to the Winterset students but never got through to most of them. She had picked Yeats partly because of what Kincaid had just said, thinking all of those qualities would appeal to teenagers whose glands were pounding like the high school marching band at football halftimes. But the bias against poetry they had picked up, the view of it as a product of unsteady masculinity, was too much even for Yeats to overcome.

She remembered Matthew Clark looking at the boy beside him and then forming his hands as if to cup them over a woman's breasts when she read, 'The golden apples of the sun.' They had snickered, and the girls in the back row with them blushed.

They would live with those attitudes all their lives. That's what had discouraged her, knowing that, and she felt compromised and alone, in spite of the outward friendliness of the community. Poets were not welcome here. The people of Madison County liked to say, compensating for their own self-imposed sense of cultural inferiority, 'This is a good place to raise kids.' And she always felt like responding, 'But is it a good place to raise adults?'

Without any conscious plan, they had walked slowly into the pasture a few hundred yards, made a loop, and were headed back toward the house. Darkness came about them as they crossed the fence, with him pushing down the wire for her this time.

She remembered the brandy. 'I have some brandy. Or would you like some coffee?'

'Is the possibility of both open?' His words came out of the darkness. She knew he was smiling.

As they came into the circle inscribed on grass and gravel by the yard light, she answered, 'Of course,' hearing the sound of something in her voice that worried her. It was the sound of easy laughter in the cafes of Naples.

It was difficult finding two cups without some kind of chip on them. Though she was sure that chipped cups were part of his life, she wanted perfect ones this time. The brandy glasses, two of them back in the cupboard, turned upside down, had never been used, like the brandy. She had to stretch on her tiptoes to reach them and was aware of her wet sandals and the jeans stretched tight across her bottom.

He sat on the same chair he had used before and watched her. The old ways. The old ways coming into him again. He wondered how her hair would feel to his touch, how the curve of her back would fit his hand, how she would feel underneath him.

The old ways struggling against all that is learned, struggling against the propriety drummed in by centuries of culture, the hard rules of civilized man. He tried to think of something else, photography or the road or covered bridges. Anything but how she looked just now.

But he failed and wondered again how it would feel to touch her skin, to put his belly against hers. The questions eternal, and always the same. The god-damned old ways, fighting toward the surface. He pounded them back, pushed them down, lit a Camel, and breathed deeply.

She could feel his eyes on her constantly, though his watching was circumspect, never obvious, never intrusive. She knew that he knew brandy had never been poured into those glasses. And with his Irishman's sense of the tragic, she also knew he felt something about such emptiness. Not pity. That was not what he was about. Sadness, maybe. She could almost hear his mind forming the words:

the bottle unopened,
and glasses empty,
she reached to find them,
somewhere north of Middle River,
in Iowa.
I watched her with eyes
that had seen a Jivaro's Amazon
and the Silk Road
with caravan dust
climbing behind me,
reaching into unused
spaces of Asian sky.

As Francesca stripped the Iowa liquor seal from the top of the brandy bottle, she looked at her fingernails and wished they were longer and better cared for. Farm life did not permit long fingernails. Until now it hadn't mattered.

Brandy, two glasses, on the table. While she arranged the coffee, he opened the bottle and poured just the right amount into each glass. Robert Kincaid had dealt with after-dinner brandy before.

She wondered in how many kitchens, how many good restaurants, how many living rooms with subdued light he had practised that small trade. How many sets of long fingernails had he watched delicately pointing toward him from the stems of brandy glasses, how many pairs of blue-round and brown-oval eyes had looked at him through foreign evenings, while anchored sailboats rocked offshore and water slapped against the quays of ancient ports?

The overhead kitchen light was too bright for coffee and brandy. Francesca Johnson, Richard Johnson's wife, would leave it on. Francesca Johnson, a woman walking through after-supper grass and leafing through girlhood dreams, would turn it off. A candle was in order, but that would be too much. He might get the wrong idea. She put on the small light over the kitchen sink and turned off the overhead. It was still not perfect, but it was better.

He raised his glass to shoulder level and moved it toward her. 'To ancient evenings and distant music.' For some reason those words made her take a short, quick breath. But she touched her glass to his, and even though she wanted to say, 'To ancient evenings and distant music,' she only smiled a little.

They both smoked, saying nothing, drinking brandy, drinking coffee. A pheasant called from the fields. Jack, the collie, barked twice out in the yard. Mosquitoes tested the window screen near the table, and a single moth, circuitous of thought yet sure of instinct, was goaded by the sink light's possibilities.

It was still hot, no breeze, some humidity now. Robert Kincaid was perspiring mildly, his top two shirt buttons undone. He was not looking at her directly, though she sensed his peripheral vision could find her, even as he seemed to stare out the window. In the way he was turned, she could see the top of his chest through the open buttons of his shirt and small beads of moisture lying there upon his skin.

Francesca was feeling good feelings, old feelings, poetry and music feelings. Still, it was time for him to go, she thought. Nine fifty-two on the clock above the refrigerator. Faron Young on the radio. Tune from a few years back. 'The Shrine of St Cecilia.' Roman martyr of the third century AD, Francesca remembered that. Patron saint of music and the blind.

His glass was empty. Just as he swung around from looking out the window, Francesca picked up the brandy bottle by the neck and gestured with it toward the empty glass. He shook his head. 'Roseman Bridge at dawn. I'd better get going.'

She was relieved. But she sank in disappointment. She turned around inside of herself. Yes, please leave. Have some more brandy. Stay. Go. Faron Young didn't care about her feelings. Neither did the moth above the sink. She didn't know for sure what Robert Kincaid thought.

He stood, swung one knapsack onto his left shoulder, put the other on top of his cooler. She came around the table. His hand moved toward her, and she took it. 'Thanks for the evening, the supper, the walk. They were all nice. You're a good person, Francesca. Keep the brandy toward the front of the cupboard; maybe it'll work out after a while.'

He had known, just as she thought. But she wasn't offended by his words. He was talking about romance, and he meant it in the best possible way. She could tell by the softness of his language, the way he said the words. What she didn't know was that he wanted to shout at the kitchen walls, bas-reliefing his words in the plaster: 'For Christ's sake, Richard Johnson, are you as big a fool as I think you must be?'

She followed him out to his truck and stood by while he put his gear into it. The collie came across the yard, sniffing around the truck. 'Jack, come here,' she whispered sharply, and the dog moved to sit by her, panting.

'Good-bye. Take care,' he said, stopping by the truck door to look at her for a moment, straight at her. Then, in one motion, he was behind the wheel and shutting the door after him. He turned the old engine over, stomped at the accelerator, and it rattled into a start. He leaned out the window, grinning, 'Tune-up required, I think.'

He let in the clutch, backed up, shifted again, and headed across the yard under the light. Just before he reached the darkness of the lane, his left hand came out of the window and waved back at her. She waved, too, even though she knew he couldn't see it.

As the truck moved down the lane, she jogged over and stood in shadow, watching the red lights rising and falling with the bumps. Robert Kincaid turned left on the main road toward Winterset, while heat lightning cut the summer sky and Jack slumbered toward the back porch.

After he left, Francesca stood before the bureau mirror, naked. Her hips flared only a little from the children, her breasts were still nice and firm, not too large, not too small, belly slightly rounded. She couldn't see her legs in the mirror, but she knew they were still good. She should shave more often, but there didn't seem much point to it.

Richard was interested in sex only occasionally, every couple of months, but it was over fast, rudimentary and unmoving, and he didn't seem to care much about perfume or shaving or any of that. It was easy to get a little sloppy.

She was more of a business partner to him than anything else. Some of her appreciated that. But rustling yet within her was another person who wanted to bathe and perfume herself ... and be taken, carried away, and peeled back by a force she could sense, but never articulate, even dimly within her mind.

She dressed again and sat at the kitchen table writing on half a sheet of plain paper. Jack followed her out to the Ford pickup and jumped in when she opened the door. He went to the passenger side and stuck his head out the window as she backed the truck out of the shed, looking over at her, then out the window again as she drove down the lane and turned right onto the county road.

Roseman Bridge was dark. But Jack loped on ahead, checking things out while she carried a flashlight from the truck. She tacked the note on the left side of the entrance to the bridge and went home.

The Bridges of Tuesday

ROBERT KINCAID DROVE past Richard Johnson's mailbox an hour before dawn, alternately chewing on a Milky Way and taking bites from an apple, squeezing the coffee cup on the seat between his thighs to keep it from tipping over. He looked up at the white house standing in thin, late moonlight as he passed and shook his head at the stupidity of men, some men, most men. They could at least drink the brandy and not bang the screen door on their way out.

Francesca heard the out-of-tune pickup go by. She lay there in bed, having slept naked for the first time as far back as she could remember. She could imagine Kincaid, hair blowing in the wind curling through the truck window, one hand on the wheel, the other holding a Camel.

She listened as the sound of his wheels faded toward Roseman Bridge. And she began to roll words over in her mind from the Yeats poem: 'I went out to the hazel wood, because a fire was in my head ....' Her rendering of it fell somewhere between that of teacher and supplicant.

He parked the truck well back from the bridge so it wouldn't interfere with his compositions. From the small space behind the seat, he took a knee-high pair of rubber boots, sitting on the running board to unlace his leather ones and pull on the others. One knapsack with straps over both shoulders, tripod slung over his left shoulder by its leather strap, the other knapsack in his right hand, he worked his way down the steep bank toward the stream.

The trick would be to put the bridge at an angle for some compositional tension, get a little of the stream at the same time, and miss the graffiti on the walls near the entrance. The telephone wires in the background were a problem, too, but that could be handled through careful framing.

He took out the Nikon loaded with Kodachrome and screwed it onto the heavy tripod. The camera had the 24-millimetre lens on it, and he replaced that with his favourite 105-millimetre. Grey light in the east now, and he began to experiment with his composition. Move tripod two feet left, readjust legs sticking in muddy ground by the stream. He kept the camera strap wound over his left wrist, a practice he always followed when working around water. He'd seen too many cameras go into the water when tripods tipped over.

Red colour coming up, sky brightening. Lower camera six inches, adjust tripod legs. Still not there. A foot more to the left. Adjust legs again. Level camera on tripod head. Set lens to f/8. Estimate depth of field, maximize it via hyperfocal technique. Screw in cable release on shutter button. Sun 40 per cent above the horizon, old paint on the bridge turning a warm red, just what he wanted.

Light meter out of left breast pocket. Check it at f/8. One-second exposure, but the Kodachrome would hold well for that extreme. Look through the view-finder. Fine-tune levelling of camera. He pushed the plunger of the shutter release and waited for a second to pass.

Just as he fired the shutter, something caught his eye. He looked through the viewfinder again. 'What the hell is hanging by the entrance to the bridge?' he muttered. 'A piece of paper. Wasn't there yesterday.'

Tripod steady. Run up the bank with sun coming fast behind him. Paper neatly tacked to bridge. Pull it off, put tack and paper in vest pocket. Back toward the bank, down it, behind the camera. Sun 60 per cent up.

Breathing hard from the sprint. Shoot again. Repeat twice for duplicates. No wind, grass still. Shoot three at two seconds and three at one-half second for insurance.

Click lens to f/16 setting. Repeat entire process. Carry tripod and camera to the middle of the stream. Get set up, silt from footsteps moving away behind. Shoot entire sequence again. New roll of Kodachrome. Switch lenses. Lock on the 24–millimetre, jam the 105 into a pocket. Move closer to the bridge, wading upstream. Adjust, level, light check, fire three, and bracket shots for insurance.

Flip the camera to vertical, recompose. Shoot again. Same sequence, methodical. There never was anything clumsy about his movements. All were practised, all had a reason, the contingencies were covered, efficiently and professionally.

Up the bank, through the bridge, running with the equipment, racing the sun. Now the tough one. Grab second camera with faster film, sling both cameras around neck, climb tree behind bridge. Scrape arm on bark—'Dammit!'—keep climbing. High up now, looking down on the bridge at an angle with the stream catching sunlight.

Use spot meter to isolate bridge roof, then shady side of bridge. Take reading off water. Set camera for compromise. Shoot nine shots, bracketing, camera resting on vest wedged into tree crotch. Switch cameras. Faster film. Shoot a dozen more shots.

Down the tree. Down the bank. Set up tripod, reload Kodachrome, shoot composition similar to the first series only from the opposite side of the stream. Pull third camera out of bag. The old S P, rangefinder camera. Black-and-white work now. Light on bridge changing second by second.

After twenty intense minutes of the kind understood only by soldiers, surgeons, and photographers, Robert Kincaid swung his knapsacks into the truck and headed back down the road he had come along before. It was fifteen minutes to Hogback Bridge northwest of town, and he might just get some shots there if he hurried.

Dust flying, Camel lit, truck bouncing, past the white frame house facing north, past Richard Johnson's mailbox. No sign of her. What did you expect? She's married, doing okay. You're doing okay. Who needs those kinds of complications? Nice evening, nice supper, nice woman. Leave it at that. God, she's lovely, though, and there's something about her. Something. I have trouble taking my eyes away from her.

Francesca was in the barn doing chores when he barrelled past her place. Noise from the livestock cloaked any sound from the road. And Robert Kincaid headed for Hogback Bridge, racing the years, chasing the light.

Things went well at the second bridge. It sat in a valley and still had mist rising around it when he arrived. The 300-millimetre lens gave him a big sun in the upper-left part of his frame, with the rest taking in the winding white rock road toward the bridge and the bridge itself.

Then into his viewfinder came a farmer driving a team of light brown Belgians pulling a wagon along the white road. One of the last of the old-style boys, Kincaid thought, grinning. He knew when the good ones came by and could already see what the final print would look like as he worked. On the vertical shots he left some light sky where a title could go.

When he folded up his tripod at eight thirty-five, he felt good. The morning's work had some keepers. Bucolic, conservative stuff, but nice and solid. The one with the farmer and horses might even be a cover shot; that's why he had left the space at the top of the frame, room for type, for a logo. Editors liked that kind of thoughtful craftsmanship. That's why Robert Kincaid got assignments.

He had shot all or part of seven rolls of film, emptied the three cameras, and reached into the lower-left pocket of his vest to get the other four. 'Damn!' The thumbtack pricked his index finger. He had forgotten about dropping it in the pocket when he'd removed the piece of paper from Roseman Bridge. In fact, he had forgotten about the piece of paper. He fished it out, opened it, and read: 'If you'd like supper again when "white moths are on the wing," come by tonight after you're finished. Anytime is fine.'

He couldn't help smiling a little, imagining Francesca Johnson with her note and thumbtack driving through the darkness to the bridge. In five minutes he was back in town. While the Texaco man filled the tank and checked the oil ('Down half a quart'), Kincaid used the pay telephone at the station. The thin phone book was grimy from being thumbed by filling station hands.

There were two listings under 'R. Johnson,' but one had a town address.

He dialled the rural number and waited. Francesca was feeding the dog on the back porch when the phone rang in the kitchen. She caught it at the front of the second ring: 'Johnson's.'

'Hi, this is Robert Kincaid.'

Her insides jumped again, just as they had yesterday. A little stab of something that started in her chest and plunged to her stomach.

'Got your note. W. B. Yeats as a messenger and all that. I accept the invitation, but it might be late. The weather's pretty good, so I'm planning on shooting the—let's see, what's it called?—the Cedar Bridge ... this evening. It could be after nine before I'm finished. Then I'll want to clean up a bit. So I might not be there until nine-thirty or ten. Is that all right?'

No, it wasn't all right. She didn't want to wait that long, but she only said, 'Oh, sure. Get your work done; that's what's important. I'll fix something that'll be easy to warm up when you get here.'

Then he added, 'If you want to come along while I'm shooting, that's fine. It won't bother me. I could stop by for you about five-thirty.'

Francesca's mind worked the problem. She wanted to go with him. But what if someone saw her? What could she say to Richard if he found out?

Cedar Bridge sat fifty yards upstream from and

parallel to the new road and its concrete bridge. She wouldn't be too noticeable. Or would she? In less than two seconds, she decided. 'Yes, I'd like that. But I'll drive my pickup and meet you there. What time?'

'About six. I'll see you then. Okay? 'Bye.'

He spent the rest of the day at the local newspaper office looking through old editions. It was a pretty town, with a nice courthouse square, and he sat there on a bench in the shade at lunch with a small sack of fruit and some bread, along with a Coke from a cafe across the street.

When he had walked in the cafe and asked for a Coke to take out, it was a little after noon. Like an old Wild West saloon when the regional gunfighter appeared, the busy conversation had stopped for a moment while they all looked him over. He hated that, felt self-conscious; but it was the standard procedure in small towns. Someone new! Someone different! Who is he? What's he doing here?

'Somebody said he's a photographer. Said they saw him out by Hogback Bridge this morning with all sorts of cameras.'

'Sign on his truck says he's from Washington, out west.'

'Been over to the newspaper office all morning. Jim says he's looking through the papers for information on the covered bridges.'

'Yeah, young Fischer at the Texaco said he stopped

in yesterday and asked directions to all the covered bridges.'

'What's he wanna know about them for, anyway?'

'And why in the world would anybody wanna take pictures of 'em? They're just all fallin' down in bad shape.'

'Sure does have long hair. Looks like one of them Beatle fellows, or what is it they been callin' some of them other people? Hippies, ain't that it?' That brought laughter in the back booth and to the table next to it.

Kincaid got his Coke and left, the eyes still on him as he went out the door. Maybe he'd made a mistake in inviting Francesca, for her sake, not his. If someone saw her at Cedar Bridge, word would hit the cafe next morning at breakfast, relayed by young Fischer at the Texaco station after taking a handoff from the passerby. Probably quicker than that.

He'd learned never to underestimate the tele-communicative flash of trivial news in small towns. Two million children could be dying of hunger in the Sudan, and that wouldn't cause a bump in consciousness. But Richard Johnson's wife seen with a long-haired stranger—now that was news! News to be passed around, news to be chewed on, news that created a vague carnal lapping in the minds of those who heard it, the only such ripple they'd feel that year.

He finished his lunch and walked over to the public phone on the parking lot of the courthouse. Dialled her number. She answered, slightly breathless, on the third ring. 'Hi, it's Robert Kincaid again.'

Her stomach tightened instantly as she thought, He can't come; he's called to say that.

'Let me be direct. If it's a problem for you to come out with me tonight, given the curiosity of small-town people, don't feel pressured to do it. Frankly, I couldn't care less what they think of me around here, and one way or the other, I'll come by later. What I'm trying to say is that I might have made an error in inviting you, so don't feel compelled in any way to do it. Though I'd love to have you along.'

She'd been thinking about just that since they'd talked earlier. But she had decided. 'No, I'd like to see you do your work. I'm not worried about talk.' She was worried, but something in her had taken hold, something to do with risk. Whatever the cost, she was going out to Cedar Bridge.

'Great. Just thought I'd check. See you later.'

'Okay.' He was sensitive, but she already knew that.

At four o'clock he stopped by his motel and did some laundry in the sink, put on a clean shirt, and tossed a second one in the truck, along with a pair of khaki slacks and brown sandals he'd picked up in India in 1962 while doing a story on the baby railroad up to Darjeeling. At a tavern he purchased two six-packs of Budweiser. Eight of the bottles, all that would fit, he arranged around his film in the cooler.

Hot, real hot again. The late afternoon sun in Iowa piled itself on top of its earlier damage, which had been absorbed by cement and brick and earth. It fairly blistered down out of the west.

The tavern had been dark and passably cool, with the front door open and big fans on the ceiling and one on a stand by the door whirring at about a hundred and five decibels. Somehow, though, the noise of the fans, the smell of stale beer and smoke, the blare of the jukebox, and the semihostile faces staring at him from along the bar made it seem hotter than it really was.

Out on the road the sunlight almost hurt, and he thought about the Cascades and fir trees and breezes along the Strait of San Juan de Fuca, near Kydaka Point.

Francesca Johnson looked cool, though. She was leaning against the fender of her Ford pickup where she had parked it behind some trees near the bridge. She had on the same jeans that fit her so well, sandals, and a white cotton T-shirt that did nice things for her body. He waved as he pulled up next to her truck.

'Hi. Nice to see you. Pretty hot,' he said. Innocuous talk, around-the-edges-of-things talk. That old uneasiness again, just being in the presence of a woman for whom he felt something. He never knew quite what to say, unless the talk was serious. Even though his sense of humour was well developed, if a little bizarre, he had a fundamentally serious mind and took things seriously.

His mother had always said he was an adult at four years of age. That served him well as a professional. To his way of thinking, though, it did not serve him well around women such as Francesca Johnson.

'I wanted to watch you make your pictures. "Shoot," as you call it.'

'Well, you're about to see it, and you'll find it pretty boring. At least other people generally do. It's not like listening to someone practise the piano, where you can be part of it. In photography, production and performance are separated by a long time span. Today I'm doing production. When the pictures appear somewhere, that's the performance. All you're going to see is a lot of fiddling around. But you're more than welcome. In fact, I'm glad you came.'

She hung on those last four words. He needn't have said them. He could have stopped with 'welcome,' but he didn't. He was genuinely glad to see her; that was clear. She hoped the fact she was here implied something of the same to him.

'Can I help you in some way?' she asked as he pulled on his rubber boots.

'You can carry that blue knapsack. I'll take the tan one and the tripod.'

So Francesca became a photographer's assistant. He had been wrong. There was much to see. There *was* a performance of sorts, though he was not aware of it. It was what she had noticed yesterday and part of what drew her toward him. His grace, his quick eyes, the muscles along his forearms working. Mostly the way he moved his body. The men she knew seemed cumbrous compared to him.

It wasn't that he hurried. In fact, he didn't hurry at all. There was a gazellelike quality about him, though she could tell he was strong in a supple way. Maybe he was more like a leopard than a gazelle. Yes. Leopard, that was it. He was not prey. Quite the reverse, she sensed.

'Francesca, give me the camera with the blue strap, please.'

She opened the knapsack, feeling a little overcautious about the expensive equipment he handled so casually, and took out the camera. It said 'Nikon' on the chrome plating of the viewfinder, with an 'F' to the upper left of the name.

He was on his knees northeast of the bridge, with the tripod low. He held out his left hand without taking his eye from the viewfinder, and she gave him the camera, watching his hand close about the lens as he felt it touch him. He worked the plunger on the end of the cord she had seen hanging out of his vest yesterday. The shutter fired. He cocked the shutter and fired again.

He reached under the tripod head and unscrewed the camera on it, which was replaced by the one she had given him. While he fastened on the new one, he turned his head toward her and grinned. 'Thanks, you're a first-class assistant.' She flushed a little.

God, what was it about him! He was like some star creature who had draughted in on the tail of a comet and dropped off at the end of her lane. Why can't I just say 'you're welcome'? she thought. I feel sort of slow around him, though it's nothing he does. It's me, not him. I'm just not used to being with people whose minds work as fast as his does.

He moved into the creek, then up the other bank. She went through the bridge with the blue knapsack and stood behind him, happy, strangely happy. There was energy here, a power of some kind in the way he worked. He didn't just wait for nature, he took it over in a gentle way, shaping it to his vision, making it fit what he saw in his mind.

He imposed his will on the scene, countering changes in light with different lenses, different films, a filter occasionally. He didn't just fight back, he dominated, using skill and intellect. Farmers also dominated the land with chemicals and bulldozers. But Robert Kincaid's way of changing nature was elastic and always left things in their original form when he finished.

She looked at the jeans pulling themselves tight around his thigh muscles as he knelt down. At the faded denim shirt sticking to his back, grey hair over the collar of it. At how he sat back on his haunches to adjust a piece of equipment, and for the first time in ever so long, she grew wet between her legs just watching someone. When she felt it, she looked up at the evening sky and breathed deeply, listening to him quietly curse a jammed filter that wouldn't unscrew from a lens.

He crossed the creek again back toward the trucks, sloshing along in his rubber boots. Francesca went into the covered bridge, and when she came out the other end, he was crouched and pointing a camera toward her. He fired, cocked the shutter, and fired a second and third time as she walked toward him along the road. She felt herself grin in mild embarrassment.

'Don't worry.' He smiled. 'I won't use those anywhere without your permission. I'm finished here. Think I'll stop by the motel and rinse off a bit before coming out.'

'Well, you can if you want. But I can spare a towel or a shower or the pump or whatever,' she said quietly, earnestly.

'Okay, you're on. Go ahead. I'll load the equipment in Harry—that's my truck—and be right there.'

She backed Richard's new Ford out of the trees and took it up on the main road away from the bridge, turned right, and headed toward Winterset, where she cut southwest toward home. The dust was too thick for her to see if he was following, though once, coming around a curve, she thought she could see his lights a mile back, rattling along in the truck he called Harry.

It must have been him, for she heard his truck coming up the lane just after she arrived. Jack barked at first but settled down right away, muttering to himself, 'Same guy as last night; okay, I guess.' Kincaid stopped for a moment to talk with him.

Francesca stepped out of the back porch door. 'Shower?'

'That'd be great. Show me the way.'

She took him upstairs to the bathroom she had insisted Richard put in when the children were growing up. That was one of the few demands on which she had stood firm. She liked long hot baths in the evening, and she wasn't going to deal with teenagers tromping around in her private spaces. Richard used the other bath, said he felt uncomfortable with all the feminine things in hers. 'Too fussy,' were his words.

The bath could be reached only through their bedroom. She opened the door to it and took out an assortment of towels and a washcloth from a cupboard under the sink. 'Use anything you want.' She smiled while biting her lower lip slightly.

'I might borrow some shampoo if you can spare it. Mine's at the motel.'

'Sure. Take your pick.' She set three different bottles on the counter, each partly used.

'Thanks.' He tossed his fresh clothes on the bed, and Francesca noted the khakis, white shirt, and sandals. None of the local men wore sandals. A few of them from town had started wearing Bermuda shorts at the golf course, but not the farmers. And sandals . . . never.

She went downstairs and heard the shower come on. He's naked now, she thought, and felt funny in her lower belly.

Earlier in the day, after he called, she had driven the forty miles into Des Moines and went to the state liquor store. She was not experienced in this and asked a clerk about a good wine. He didn't know any more than she did, which was nothing. So she looked through the rows of bottles until she came across a label that read 'Valpolicella.' She remembered that from a long time ago. Dry, Italian red wine. She bought two bottles and another decanter of brandy, feeling sensual and worldly.

Next she looked for a new summer dress from a shop downtown. She found one, light pink with thin straps. It scooped down at the back, did the same in front rather dramatically so the tops of her breasts were exposed, and gathered around her waist with a narrow sash. And new white sandals, expensive ones, flat-heeled, with delicate handiwork on the straps.

In the afternoon she fixed stuffed peppers, filling them with a mixture of tomato sauce, brown rice, cheese, and chopped parsley. Then came a simple spinach salad, corn bread, and an applesauce soufflé for dessert. All of it, except the soufflé, went into the refrigerator.

She hurried to shorten her dress to knee length. The Des Moines *Register* had carried an article earlier in the summer saying that was the preferred length this year. She always had thought fashion and all it implied pretty

101

weird, people behaving sheeplike in the service of European designers. But the length suited her, so that's where the hem went.

The wine was a problem. People around here kept it in the refrigerator, though in Italy they never had done that. Yet it was too warm just to let it sit on the counter. Then she remembered the spring house. It was about sixty degrees in there in the summer, so she put the wine along the wall.

The shower shut off upstairs just as the phone rang. It was Richard, calling from Illinois.

'Everything okay?'

'Yes.'

'Carolyn's steer'll be judged on Wednesday. Some other things we want to see next day. Be home Friday, late.'

'All right, have a good time and drive carefully.'

'Frannie, you sure you're okay? Sound a little strange.'

'No, I'm fine. Just hot. I'll be better after my bath.'

'Okay. Say hello to Jack for me.'

'Yes, I'll do that.' She glanced at Jack sprawled on the cement of the back porch floor.

Robert Kincaid came down the stairs and into the kitchen. White button-down-collar shirt, sleeves rolled up to just above the elbow, light khaki slacks, brown sandals, silver bracelet, top two buttons of his shirt open, silver chain. His hair was still damp and brushed neatly, with a parting in the middle. And she marvelled at the sandals.

'I'll just take my field duds out to the truck and bring in the gear for a little cleaning.'

'Go ahead. I'm going to take a bath.'

'Want a beer with your bath?'

'If you have an extra one.'

He brought in the cooler first, lifted out a beer for her, and opened it, while she found two tall glasses that would serve as mugs. When he went back to the truck for the cameras, she took her beer and went upstairs, noted that he had cleaned the tub, and then ran a high, warm bath for herself, settling in with her glass on the floor beside her while she shaved and soaped. He had been here just a few minutes before; she was lying where the water had run down his body, and she found that intensely erotic. Almost everything about Robert Kincaid had begun to seem erotic to her.

Something as simple as a cold glass of beer at bath time felt so elegant. Why didn't she and Richard live this way? Part of it, she knew, was the inertia of protracted custom. All marriages, all relationships, are susceptible to that. Custom brings predictability, and predictability carries its own comforts; she was aware of that, too.

And there was the farm. Like a demanding invalid, it needed constant attention, even though the steady substitution of equipment for human labour had made much of the work less onerous than it had been in the past.

But there was something more going on here. Predictability is one thing, fear of change is something else. And Richard was afraid of change, any kind of change, in their marriage. Didn't want to talk about it in general. Didn't want to talk about sex in particular. Eroticism was, in some way, dangerous business, unseemly to his way of thinking.

But he wasn't alone and really wasn't to blame. What was the barrier to freedom that had been erected out here? Not just on their farm, but in the rural culture. Maybe urban culture, for that matter. Why the walls and the fences preventing open, natural relationships between men and women? Why the lack of intimacy, the absence of eroticism?

The women's magazines talked about these matters. And women were starting to have expectations about their allotted place in the grander scheme of things, as well as what transpired in the bedrooms of their lives. Men such as Richard—most men, she guessed—were threatened by these expectations. In a way, women were asking for men to be poets and driving, passionate lovers at the same time.

Women saw no contradiction in that. Men did. The locker rooms and stag parties and pool halls and segregated gatherings of their lives defined a certain set of male characteristics in which poetry, or anything of subtlety, had no place. Hence, if eroticism was a matter of subtlety, an art form of its own, which Francesca knew it to be, it had no place in the fabric of their lives. So the distracting and conveniently clever dance that held them apart went on, while women sighed and turned their faces to the wall in the nights of Madison County.

There was something in the mind of Robert Kincaid that understood all of this, implicitly. She was sure of that.

Walking into the bedroom, towelling off, she noted it was a little after ten. Still hot, but the bath had cooled her. From the closet she took the new dress.

She pulled her long black hair behind her and fastened it with a silver clasp. Silver earrings, large hooped ones, and a loose-fitting silver bracelet also she had bought in Des Moines that morning.

The Wind Song perfume again. A little lipstick on the high-cheekboned, Latin face, the shade of pink even lighter than the dress. Her tan from working outdoors in shorts and midriff tops accented the whole outfit. Her slim legs came out from under the hem looking just fine.

She turned first one way, then the other, looking at herself in the bureau mirror. That's about as good as I can do, she thought. And then, pleased, said half out loud, 'It's pretty good, though.'

Robert Kincaid was working on his second beer and

repacking the cameras when she came into the kitchen. He looked up at her.

'Jesus,' he said softly. All of the feelings, all of the searching and reflecting, a lifetime of feeling and searching and reflecting, came together at that moment. And he fell in love with Francesca Johnson, farmer's wife, of Madison County, Iowa, long ago from Naples.

'I mean'—his voice was a little shaky, a little rough—'if you don't mind my boldness, you look stunning. Make-'em-run-around-the-block-howling-in-agony stunning. I'm serious. You're big-time elegant, Francesca, in the purest sense of that word.'

His admiration was genuine, she could tell. She revelled in it, bathed in it, let it swirl over her and into the pores of her skin like soft oil from the hands of some deity somewhere who had deserted her years ago and had now returned.

And, in the catch of that moment, she fell in love with Robert Kincaid, photographer-writer, from Bellingham, Washington, who drove an old pickup truck named Harry.

Room to Dance Again

On that Tuesday evening in August of 1965, Robert Kincaid looked steadily at Francesca Johnson. She looked back in kind. From ten feet apart they were locked in to one another, solidly, intimately, and inextricably.

The telephone rang. Still looking at him, she did not move on the first ring, or the second. In the long silence after the second ring, and before the third, he took a deep breath and looked down at his camera bags. With that she was able to move across the kitchen toward the phone hanging on the wall just behind his chair.

'Johnson's. ... Hi, Marge. Yes, I'm fine. Thursday night?' She calculated: He said he'd be here a week, he came yesterday, this is only Tuesday. The decision to lie was an easy one.

She was standing by the door to the porch, phone in her left hand. He sat within touching distance, his back to her. She reached out with her right hand and rested it on his shoulder, in the casual way that some women have with men they care for. In only twenty-four hours she had come to care for Robert Kincaid.

'Oh, Marge, I'm tied up then. I'm going shopping in Des Moines. Good chance to get a lot of things done I've been putting off. You know, with Richard and the kids gone.'

Her hand lay quietly upon him. She could feel the muscle running from his neck along his shoulder, just back of his collarbone. She was looking down on the thick grey hair, neatly parted. Saw how it drifted over his collar. Marge babbled on.

'Yes, Richard called a little while ago. ... No, the judging's not till Wednesday, tomorrow. Richard said it'd be late Friday before they're home. Something they want to see on Thursday. It's a long drive, particularly in the stock truck. ... No, football practice doesn't start for another week. Uh-huh, a week. At least that's what Michael said.'

She was conscious of how warm his body felt through the shirt. The warmth came into her hand, moved up her arm, and from there spread through her to wherever it wanted to go, with no effort—indeed, with no control—from her. He was still, not wanting to make any noise that might cause Marge to wonder. Francesca understood this.

'Oh, yes, that was a man asking directions.' As she guessed, Floyd Clark had gone right home and told his wife about the green pickup he had seen in the Johnsons' yard on his way by yesterday.

'A photographer? Gosh, I don't know. I didn't pay much attention. Could have been.' The lies were coming easier now.

'He was looking for Roseman Bridge. ... Is that right? Taking pictures of the old bridges, huh? Oh, well, that's harmless enough.

'Hippie?' Francesca giggled and watched Kincaid's head shake slowly back and forth. 'Well, I'm not sure what a hippie looks like. This fellow was polite. He only stayed a minute or two and then was gone. ... I don't know whether they have hippies in Italy, Marge. I haven't been there for eight years. Besides, like I said, I'm not sure I'd know a hippie if I saw one.'

Marge was talking on about free love and communes and drugs she'd read about somewhere. 'Marge, I was just getting ready to step into my bath when you called, so I'd better run before the water gets cold. ... Okay, I'll call soon. 'Bye.'

She disliked removing her hand from his shoulder, but there was no good excuse not to remove it. So she walked to the sink and turned on the radio. More country music. She adjusted the dial until the sound of a big band came on and left it there.

'"Tangerine,"' he said.

'What?'

'The song. It's called "Tangerine." It's about an Argentinian woman.' Talking around the edges of things again. Saying anything, anything. Fighting for time and the sense of it all, hearing somewhere at the back of his mind the faint click of a door shutting behind two people in an Iowa kitchen.

She smiled softly at him. 'Are you hungry? I have supper ready whenever you want.'

'It was a long, good day. I wouldn't mind another beer before I eat. Will you have one with me?' Stalling, looking for his centre, losing it moment by moment.

She would. He opened two and set one on her side of the table.

Francesca was pleased with how she looked and how she felt. Feminine. That's how she felt. Light and warm and feminine. She sat on the kitchen chair, crossed her legs, and the hem of her skirt rode up well above her right knee. Kincaid was leaning against the refrigerator, arms folded across his chest, Budweiser in his right hand. She was pleased that he noticed her legs, and he did.

He noticed all of her. He could have walked out on this earlier, could still walk. Rationality shrieked at him. 'Let it go, Kincaid, get back on the road. Shoot the bridges, go to India. Stop in Bangkok on the way and look up the silk merchant's daughter who knows every ecstatic secret the old ways can teach. Swim naked with her at dawn in jungle pools and listen to her scream as you turn her inside out at twilight. Let go of this'—the voice was hissing now—'it's outrunning you.'

But the slow street tango had begun. Somewhere it played; he could hear it, an old accordion. It was far back, or far ahead, he couldn't be sure. Yet it moved toward him steadily. And the sound of it blurred his criteria and funnelled down his alternatives toward unity. Inexorably it did that, until there was nowhere left to go, except toward Francesca Johnson.

'We could dance, if you like. The music's pretty good for it,' he said in that serious, shy way of his. Then he quickly tacked on his caveat: 'I'm not much of a dancer, but if you'd like to, I can probably handle it in a kitchen.'

Jack scratched at the porch door, wanting in. He could stay out.

Francesca blushed only a little. 'Okay. But I don't dance much, either ... anymore. I did as a young girl in Italy, but now it's just pretty much on New Year's Eve, and then only a little bit.'

He smiled and put his beer on the counter. She rose, and they moved toward each other. 'It's your Tuesday night dance party from WGN, Chicago,' said the smooth baritone. 'We'll be back after these messages.'

They both laughed. Telephones and commercials. Something there was that kept inserting reality between them. They knew it without saying it.

But he had reached out and taken her right hand anyway, in his left. He leaned easily against the counter, legs crossed at the ankles, right one on top. She rested beside him, against the sink, and looked out the window near the table, feeling his slim fingers around her hand. There was no breeze, and the corn was growing.

'Oh, just a minute.' She reluctantly removed her hand from his and opened the bottom right cupboard. From it she took two white candles she had bought in Des Moines that morning, along with a small brass holder for each candle. She put them on the table.

He walked over, tilted each one, and lit it, while she snapped off the overhead light. It was dark now, except for the small flames pointing straight upward, barely fluttering on a windless night. The plain kitchen had never looked this good.

The music started again. Fortunately for both of them, it was a slow rendition of 'Autumn Leaves.'

She felt awkward. So did he. But he took her hand, put an arm around her waist, she moved into him, and the awkwardness vanished. Somehow it worked in an easy kind of way. He moved his arm farther around her waist and pulled her closer.

She could smell him, clean and soaped and warm. A good, fundamental smell of a civilized man who seemed, in some part of himself, aboriginal.

'Nice perfume,' he said, bringing their hands in to lie upon his chest, near his shoulder.

'Thank you.'

They danced, slowly. Not moving very far in any

direction. She could feel his legs against hers, their stomachs touching occasionally.

The song ended, but he held on to her, hummed the melody that had just played, and they stayed as they were until the next song began. He automatically led her into it, and the dance went on, while locusts complained about the coming of September.

She could feel the muscles of his shoulder through the light cotton shirt. He was real, more real than anything she'd ever known. He bent slightly to put his cheek against hers.

During the time they spent together, he once referred to himself as one of the last cowboys. They had been sitting on the grass by the pump out back. She didn't understand and asked him about it.

'There's a certain breed of man that's obsolete,' he had said. 'Or very nearly so. The world is getting organized, way too organized for me and some others. Everything in its place, a place for everything. Well, my camera equipment is pretty well organized, I admit, but I'm talking about something more than that. Rules and regulations and laws and social conventions. Hierarchies of authority, spans of control, long-range plans, and budgets. Corporate power; in "Bud" we trust. A world of wrinkled suits and stick-on name tags.

'Not all men are the same. Some will do okay in the world that's coming. Some, maybe just a few of us, will not. You can see it in computers and robots and what

115

they portend. In older worlds, there were things we could do, were designed to do, that nobody or no machine could do. We run fast, are strong and quick, aggressive and tough. We were given courage. We can throw spears long distances and fight in hand-to-hand combat.

'Eventually, computers and robots will run things. Humans will manage those machines, but that doesn't require courage or strength, or any characteristics like those. In fact, men are outliving their usefulness. All you need are sperm banks to keep the species going, and those are coming along now. Most men are rotten lovers, women say, so there's not much loss in replacing sex with science.

'We're giving up free range, getting organized, feathering our emotions. Efficiency and effectiveness and all those other pieces of intellectual artifice. And with the loss of free range, the cowboy disappears, along with the mountain lion and grey wolf. There's not much room left for travellers.

'I'm one of the last cowboys. My job gives me free range of a sort. As much as you can find nowadays. I'm not sad about it. Maybe a little wistful, I guess. But it's got to happen; it's the only way we'll keep from destroying ourselves. My contention is that male hormones are the ultimate cause of trouble on this planet. It was one thing to dominate another tribe or another warrior. It's quite another to have missiles. It's also quite another to have the power to destroy nature the way we're doing. Rachel Carson is right. So were John Muir and Aldo Leopold.

'The curse of modern times is the preponderance of male hormones in places where they can do long-term damage. Even if we're not talking about wars between nations or assaults on nature, there's still that aggressiveness that keeps us apart from each other and the problems we need to be working on. We have to somehow sublimate those male hormones, or at least get them under control.

'It's probably time to put away the things of childhood and grow up. Hell, I recognize it. I admit it. I'm just trying to make some good pictures and get out of life before I'm totally obsolete or do some serious damage.'

Over the years, she had thought about what he'd said. It seemed right to her, somehow, on the surface of it. Yet the ways of him contradicted what he said. He had a certain plunging aggressiveness to him, but he seemed to be able to control it, to turn it on and then let go of it when he wanted. And that's what had both confused and attracted her—incredible intensity, but controlled, metered, arrowlike intensity that was mixed with warmth and no hint of meanness.

On that Tuesday night, gradually and without design, they had moved closer and closer together, dancing in the kitchen. Francesca was pressed close against his chest, and she wondered if he could feel her breasts through the dress and his shirt and was certain he could.

He felt so good to her. She wanted this to run forever. More old songs, more dancing, more of his body against hers. She had become a woman again. There was room to dance again. In a slow, unremitting way, she was turning for home, toward a place she'd never been.

It was hot. The humidity was up, and thunder rolled far in the southwest. Moths plastered themselves on the screens, looking in at the candles, chasing the fire.

He was falling into her now. And she into him. She moved her cheek away from his, looked up at him with dark eyes, and he kissed her, and she kissed back, longtime soft kissing, a river of it.

They gave up the pretence of dancing, and her arms went around his neck. His left hand was on her waist behind her back, the other brushing across her neck and her cheek and her hair. Thomas Wolfe talked about the 'ghost of the old eagerness.' The ghost had stirred in Francesca Johnson. In both of them.

Sitting by the window on her sixty-seventh birthday, Francesca watched the rain and remembered. She carried her brandy into the kitchen and stopped for a moment, staring at the exact spot where the two of them had stood. The feelings inside of her were over-whelming; they always were. Strong enough that over the years she had dared do this in detail only once a year or her mind somehow would have disintegrated at the sheer emotional bludgeoning of it all.

Her abstinence from her recollections had been a matter of survival. Though in the last few years, the detail was coming back more and more often. She had ceased trying to stop him from coming into her. The images were clear, and real, and present. And so far back. Twenty-two years back. But slowly they were becoming her reality once again, the only one in which she cared to live.

She knew she was sixty-seven and accepted it, but she could not imagine Robert Kincaid being nearly seventy-five. Could not think of it, could not conceive of it or even conceive of the conceiving of it. He was here with her, right in this kitchen, in his white shirt, long grey hair, khaki slacks, brown sandals, silver bracelet, and silver chain around his neck. He was here with his arms around her.

She finally pulled back from him, from where they stood in the kitchen, and took his hand, leading him toward the stairs, up the stairs, past Carolyn's room, past Michael's room, and into her room, turning on a small reading lamp by the bed.

Now, all these years later, Francesca carried her brandy and walked slowly up the stairs, her right hand trailing behind her to bring along the memory of him up the stairs and down the hallway into the bedroom.

The physical images were inscribed in her mind so

clearly that they might have been razor-edged photographs of his. She remembered the dreamlike sequence of clothes coming off and the two of them naked in bed. She remembered how he held himself just above her and moved his chest slowly against her belly and across her breasts. How he did this again and again, like some animal courting rite in an old zoology text. As he moved over her, he alternately kissed her lips or ears or ran his tongue along her neck, licking her as some fine leopard might do in long grass out on the veld.

He was an animal. A graceful, hard, male animal who did nothing overtly to dominate her yet dominated her completely, in the exact way she wanted that to happen at this moment.

But it was far beyond the physical, though the fact that he could make love for a long time without tiring was part of it. Loving him was—it sounded almost trite to her now, given the attention paid to such matters over the last two decades—spiritual. It was spiritual, but it wasn't trite.

In the midst of it, the lovemaking, she had whispered it to him, captured it in one sentence. 'Robert, you're so powerful it's frightening.' He *was* powerful physically, but he used his strength carefully. It was more than that, however.

Sex was one thing. In the time since she'd met him, she had settled into the anticipation—the possibility, anyway—of something pleasurable, a breaking with a routine of hammering sameness. She hadn't counted on his curious power.

It was almost as if he had taken possession of her, in all of her dimensions. That's what was frightening. She never had doubted at the beginning that one part of her could remain aloof from whatever she and Robert Kincaid did, the part that belonged to her family and life in Madison County.

But he simply took it away, all of it. She should have known when he first stepped out of his truck to ask directions. He had seemed shamanlike then, and her original judgment was correct.

They would make love for an hour, maybe more, then he would pull slowly away and look at her, lighting a cigarette and one for her. Or sometimes he would just lie beside her, always with one hand moving on her body. Then he was inside her again, whispering soft words into her ear as he loved her, kissing her between phrases, between words, his arm around her waist, pulling her into him and him into her.

And she would begin to turn in her mind, breathing heavier, letting him take her where he lived, and he lived in strange, haunted places, far back along the stems of Darwin's logic.

With her face buried in his neck and her skin against his, she could smell rivers and woodsmoke, could hear steaming trains chuffing out of winter stations in long-ago nighttimes, could see travellers in black robes moving steadily along frozen rivers and through summer meadows, beating their way toward the end of things. The leopard swept over her, again and again and yet again, like a long prairie wind, and rolling beneath him, she rode on that wind like some temple virgin toward the sweet, compliant fires marking the soft curve of oblivion.

And she murmured, softly, breathlessly, 'Oh, Robert ... Robert ... I am losing myself.'

She, who had ceased having orgasms years ago, had them in long sequences now with a half-man, half-something-else creature. She wondered about him and his endurance, and he told her that he could reach those places in his mind as well as physically, and that the orgasms of the mind had their own special character.

She had no idea what he meant. All she knew was that he had pulled in a tether of some kind and wound it around both of them so tightly she would have suffocated had it not been for the vaulting freedom from herself she felt.

The night went on, and the great spiral dance continued. Robert Kincaid discarded all sense of anything linear and moved to a part of himself that dealt only with shape and sound and shadow. Down the paths of the old ways he went, finding his direction by candles of sunlit frost melting upon the grass of summer and the red leaves of autumn.

And he heard the words he whispered to her, as if a

voice other than his own were saying them. Fragments of a Rilke poem, 'around the ancient tower ... I have been circling for a thousand years.' The lines to a Navajo sun chant. He whispered to her of the visions she brought to him—of blowing sand and magenta winds and brown pelicans riding the backs of dolphins moving north along the coast of Africa.

Sounds, small, unintelligible sounds, came from her mouth as she arched herself toward him. But it was a language he understood completely, and in this woman beneath him, with his belly against hers, deep inside her, Robert Kincaid's long search came to an end.

And he knew finally the meaning of all the small footprints on all the deserted beaches he had ever walked, of all the secret cargoes carried by ships that had never sailed, of all the curtained faces that had watched him pass down winding streets of twilight cities. And, like a great hunter of old who has travelled distant miles and now sees the light of his home campfires, his loneliness dissolved. At last. At last. He had come so far ... so far. And he lay upon her, perfectly formed and unalterably complete in his love for her. At last.

Toward morning, he raised himself slightly and said, looking straight into her eyes, 'This is why I'm here on this planet, at this time, Francesca. Not to travel or make pictures, but to love you. I know that now. I have been falling from the rim of a great, high place, somewhere back in time, for many more years than I have lived in this life. And through all of those years, I have been falling toward you.'

When they came downstairs, the radio was still on. Dawn had come up, but the sun lay behind a thin cloud cover.

'Francesca, I have a favour to ask.' He smiled at her as she fussed with the coffeepot.

'Yes?' She looked at him. Oh, God, I love him so, she thought, unsteady, wanting even more of him, never stopping.

'Slip on the jeans and T-shirt you wore last night, along with a pair of sandals. Nothing else. I want to make a picture of you as you look this morning. A photograph just for the two of us.'

She went upstairs, her legs weak from being wrapped around him all night, dressed, and went outside with him to the pasture. That's where he had made the photograph she looked at each year.

The Highway and the Peregrine

ROBERT KINCAID GAVE up photography for the next few days. And except for the necessary chores, which she minimized, Francesca Johnson gave up farm life. The two of them spent all their time together, either talking or making love. Twice, when she asked, he played the guitar and sang for her in a voice somewhere between fair and good, a little uncomfortable, telling her she was his first audience. When he said that, she smiled and kissed him, then lay back upon her feelings, listening to him sing of whaling ships and desert winds.

She rode with him in Harry to the Des Moines airport, where he shipped film to New York. He always sent the first few rolls ahead, when it was possible, so the editors could look at what he was getting and the technicians could check to make sure his camera shutters were functioning properly.

Afterward he took her to a fancy restaurant for lunch and held her hands across the table, looking at her in his intense way. And the waiter smiled, just watching

127

them, hoping he would feel that way sometime.

She marvelled at the sense Robert Kincaid had of his ways coming to a close and the ease with which he accepted it. He could see the approaching death of cowboys and others like them, including himself. And she began to understand what he meant when he said he was at the terminus of a branch of evolution and that it was a dead end. Once, in talking about what he called 'last things,' he whispered: '"Never again," cried the High-Desert Master. "Never and never and never again."' He saw nothing beyond himself along the branch. His kind was obsolete.

On Thursday they talked after making love in the afternoon. Both of them knew this conversation had to occur. Both of them had been avoiding it.

'What are we going to do?' he said.

She was silent, torn-apart silent. Then, 'I don't know,' softly.

'Look, I'll stay here if you want, or in town, or wherever. When your family comes home, I'll simply talk with your husband and explain how it lies. It won't be easy, but I'll get it done.'

She shook her head. 'Richard could never get his arms around this; he doesn't think in these terms. He doesn't understand magic and passion and all those other things we talk about and experience, and he never will. That doesn't necessarily make him an inferior person. It's just too far removed from anything he's ever felt or thought about. He has no way of dealing with it.'

'Are we going to let all of this go, then?' He was serious, not smiling.

'I don't know that, either. Robert, in a curious way, you own me. I didn't want to be owned, didn't need it, and I know you didn't intend that, but that's what has happened. I'm no longer sitting next to you, here on the grass. You have me inside of you as a willing prisoner.'

He replied, 'I'm not sure you're inside of me, or that I am inside of you, or that I own you. At least I don't want to own you. I think we're both inside of another being we have created called "us."'

'Well, we're really not inside of that being. We *are* that being. We have both lost ourselves and created something else, something that exists only as an inter-lacing of the two of us. Christ, we're in love. As deeply, as profoundly, as it's possible to be in love.

'Come travel with me, Francesca. That's not a problem. We'll make love in desert sand and drink brandy on balconies in Mombasa, watching dhows from Arabia run up their sails in the first wind of morning. I'll show you lion country and an old French city on the Bay of Bengal where there's a wonderful rooftop restaurant, and trains that climb through mountain passes and little inns run by Basques high in the Pyrenees. In a tiger preserve in south India, there's a special place on an island in the middle of a huge lake.

129

If you don't like the road, I'll set up shop somewhere and shoot local stuff or portraits or whatever it takes to keep us going.'

'Robert, when we were making love last night, you said something that I still remember. I kept whispering to you about your power—and, my God, you have that. You said, "I am the highway and a peregrine and all the sails that ever went to sea." You were right. That's what you feel; you feel the road inside of you. No, more than that, in a way that I'm not certain I can explain, you are the road. In the crack where illusion meets reality, that's where you are, out there on the road, and the road is you.

'You're old knapsacks and a truck named Harry and jet aeroplanes to Asia. And that's what I want you to be. If your evolutionary branch is a dead end, as you say it is, then I want you to hit that end at full speed. I'm not sure you can do that with me along. Don't you see, I love you so much that I cannot think of restraining you for a moment. To do that would be to kill the wild, magnificent animal that is you, and the power would die with it.'

He started to speak, but Francesca stopped him.

'Robert, I'm not quite finished. If you took me in your arms and carried me to your truck and forced me to go with you, I wouldn't murmur a complaint. You could do the same thing just by talking to me. But I don't think you will. You're too sensitive, too aware of my feelings, for that. And I have feelings of responsibility here.

'Yes, it's boring in its way. My life, that is. It lacks romance, eroticism, dancing in the kitchen to candle-light, and the wonderful feel of a man who knows how to love a woman. Most of all, it lacks you. But there's this damn sense of responsibility I have. To Richard, to the children. Just my leaving, taking away my physical presence, would be hard enough for Richard. That alone might destroy him.

'On top of that, and this is even worse, he would have to live the rest of his life with the whispers of the people here. "That's Richard Johnson. His hot little Italian wife ran off with some long-haired photographer a few years back." Richard would have to suffer that, and the children would hear the snickering of Winterset for as long as they live here. They would suffer, too. And they would hate me for it.

'As much as I want you and want to be with you and part of you, I can't tear myself away from the realness of my responsibilities. If you force me, physically or mentally, to go with you, as I said earlier, I cannot fight that. I don't have the strength, given my feelings for you. In spite of what I said about not taking the road away from you, I'd go because of my own selfish wanting of you.

'But please don't make me. Don't make me give this up, my responsibilities. I cannot do that and live with the thought of it. If I did leave now, those thoughts would turn me into something other than the woman you have come to love.'

Robert Kincaid was silent. He knew what she was saying about the road and responsibilities and how the guilt could transform her. He knew she was right, in a way. Looking out the window, he fought within himself, fought to understand her feelings. She began to cry.

Then they held each other for a long time. And he whispered to her, 'I have one thing to say, one thing only; I'll never say it another time, to anyone, and I ask you to remember it: In a universe of ambiguity, this kind of certainty comes only once, and never again, no matter how many lifetimes you live.'

They made love again that night, Thursday night, lying together until well after sunrise, touching and whispering. Francesca slept a little then, and when she awoke, the sun was high and already hot. She heard one of Harry's doors creaking and threw on some clothes.

He had made coffee and was sitting at the kitchen table, smoking, when she got there. He grinned at her. She moved across the room and buried her face in his neck, her hands in his hair, his arms around her waist. He turned her around and sat her on his lap, touching her.

Finally he stood. He had his old jeans on, with orange suspenders running over a clean khaki shirt, his Red Wing boots were laced tight, the Swiss Army knife was on his belt. His photo vest hung from the back of the chair, the cable release poking out of a pocket. The cowboy was saddled up.

'I'd better be going.'

She nodded, beginning to cry. She saw the tears in his eyes, but he kept smiling that little smile of his.

'Is it okay if I write you sometime? I want to at least send a photo or two.'

'It's all right,' Francesca said, wiping her eyes on the towel hanging from the cupboard door. 'I'll make some excuse for getting mail from a hippie photographer, as long as it's not too much.'

'You have my Washington address and phone, right?' She nodded. 'If I'm not there, call the *National Geographic* offices. Here, I'll write the number down for you.' He wrote on the pad by the phone, tore off the sheet, and handed it to her.

'Or you can always find the number in the magazine. Ask for the editorial offices. They know where I am most of the time.

'Don't hesitate if you want to see me, or just to talk. Call me collect anywhere in the world; the charges won't appear on your bill that way. And I'll be around here for a few more days. Think about what I've said. I can be here, settle the matter in short order, and we could drive northwest together.'

Francesca said nothing. She knew he could, indeed, settle the matter in short order. Richard was five years younger than him, but no match intellectually or physically for Robert Kincaid.

He slipped into his vest. Her mind was gone, empty, turning. 'Don't leave, Robert Kincaid,' she could hear herself crying out from somewhere inside.

Taking her hand, he walked through the back door toward the truck. He opened the driver's door, put his foot on the running board, then stepped off it and held her again for several minutes. Neither of them spoke; they simply stood there, sending, receiving, imprinting the feel of each on the other, indelibly. Reaffirming the existence of that special being he had talked about.

For the last time, he let her go and stepped into the truck, sitting there with the door open. Tears running down his cheeks. Tears running down her cheeks. Slowly he pulled the door shut, hinges creaking. Harry was reluctant to start, as usual, but she could hear his boot hitting the accelerator, and the old truck eventually relented.

He shifted into reverse and sat there with the clutch in. First serious, then with a little grin, pointing toward the lane. 'The road, you know. I'll be in southeast India next month. Want a card from there?'

She couldn't speak but said no with a shake of her head. That would be too much for Richard to find in the mailbox. She knew Robert understood. He nodded.

The truck backed into the farmyard, crunching across

the gravel, chickens scattering from under its wheels. Jack chased one of them into the machine shed, barking.

Robert Kincaid waved to her through the open passenger-side window. She could see the sun flashing off his silver bracelet. The top two buttons of his shirt were open.

He moved into the lane and down it. Francesca kept wiping her eyes, trying to see, the sunlight making strange prisms from her tears. As she had done the first night they met, she hurried to the head of the lane and watched the old pickup bounce along. At the end of it, the truck stopped, the driver's door swung open, and he stepped out on the running board. He could see her a hundred yards back, looking small from this distance.

He stood there, with Harry turning over impatiently in the heat, and stared. Neither of them moved; they had already said good-bye. They just looked—the Iowa farm wife, the creature at the end of his evolutionary branch, one of the last cowboys. For thirty seconds he stood there, his photographer's eyes missing nothing, making their own image that he never would lose.

He closed the door, ground the gears, and was crying again as he turned left on the county road toward Winterset. He looked back just before a grove of trees on the northwest edge of the farm would block his view and saw her sitting crosslegged in the dust where the lane began, her head in her hands.

Richard and the children arrived in early evening with stories of the fair and a ribbon the steer had won before being sold for slaughter. Carolyn was on the phone immediately. It was Friday, and Michael took the pickup truck into town for the things that seventeen-year-old boys do on Friday nights—mostly hang around the square and talk or shout at girls going by in cars. Richard turned on the television, telling Francesca how good the cornbread was as he ate a piece with butter and maple syrup.

She sat on the front porch swing. Richard came out after his programme was finished at ten o'clock. He stretched and said, 'Sure is good to be home.' Then, looking at her, 'You okay, Frannie? You seem a little tired or dreamy or somethin'.'

'Yes, I'm just fine, Richard. It's good to have you back safe and sound.'

'Well, I'm turnin' in; it's been a long week at the fair, and I'm bushed. You comin', Frannie?'

'Not for a little bit. It's kind of nice out here, so I think I'll just sit awhile.' She was tired, but she was also afraid Richard might have sex in mind. She just couldn't handle that tonight.

She could hear him walking around in their bedroom, above where she pushed back and forth on the swing, her bare feet on the porch floor. From the back of the house, she could hear Carolyn's radio playing.

She avoided going into town for the next few days,

aware all the time that Robert Kincaid was only a few miles away. Frankly, she didn't think she could stop herself if she saw him. She might run to him and say, 'Now! We must go now!' She had defied risk to see him at Cedar Bridge, now there was too much risk in seeing him again.

By Tuesday the groceries were running low and Richard needed a part for the corn picker he was getting back in shape. The day was low-slung, steady rain, light fog, cool for August.

Richard got his part and had coffee with the other men at the cafe while she shopped for groceries. He knew her schedule and was waiting out in front of the Super Value when she finished. He jumped out, wearing his Allis-Chalmers cap, and helped her load the bags into the Ford pickup, on the seat and around her knees. And she thought of tripods and knapsacks.

'I've got to run up to the implement place again. I forgot one more piece I might need.'

They drove north on U.S. Route 169, which formed the main street of Winterset. A block south of the Texaco station, she saw Harry rolling away from the pumps, windshield wipers slapping, and out onto the road ahead of them.

Their momentum brought them up right behind the old pickup, and sitting high in the Ford, she could see a black tarpaulin lashed down tight in the back, outlining a suitcase and guitar case wedged in next to the spare tyre lying flat. The back window was rain-spattered, but part of his head was visible. He leaned over as if to get something from the glove box; eight days ago he'd done that and his arm had brushed across her leg. A week ago she'd been in Des Moines buying a pink dress.

'That truck's a long way from home,' remarked Richard. 'Washington State. Looks like a woman driving it; long hair, anyway. On second thought, I'll bet it's that photographer they been talkin' about at the cafe.'

They followed Robert Kincaid a few blocks north to where 169 intersected with 92 running east and west. It was a four-way stop, with heavy cross traffic in all directions, complicated by the rain and the fog, which had got heavier.

For maybe twenty seconds they sat there. He was up ahead, only thirty feet from her. She could still do it. Get out and run to Harry's right door, climb in over the knapsacks and cooler and tripods.

Since Robert Kincaid had driven away from her last Friday, she realized, in spite of how much she thought she'd cared for him then, she had nonetheless badly underestimated her feelings. That didn't seem possible, but it was true. She had begun to understand what he already understood.

But she sat frozen by her responsibilities, staring at that back window harder than she had ever looked at anything in her life. His left signal light came on. In a moment he'd be gone. Richard was fiddling with the Ford's radio.

She began to see things in slow motion, some curious trick of the mind. His turn came, and ... slowly ... slowly ... he moved Harry into the intersection—she could visualize his long legs working the clutch and accelerator and the muscles in his right forearm flexing as he shifted gears—curling left now onto 92 toward Council Bluffs, the Black Hills, and the Northwest ... slowly ... slowly ... the old pickup came around ... so slowly it came around through the intersection, putting its nose to the west.

Squinting through tears and rain and fog, she could barely make out the faded red paint on the door: 'Kincaid Photography—Bellingham, Washington.'

He had lowered his window to help him get through the bad visibility as he turned. He made the corner, and she could see his hair blowing as he began to accelerate down 92, heading west, rolling up the window as he drove.

'Oh, Christ—oh, Jesus Christ Almighty ... no!' The words were inside of her. 'I was wrong, Robert, I was wrong to stay ... but I can't go. ... Let me tell you again ... why I can't go. ... Tell me again why I should go.'

And she heard his voice coming back down the highway. 'In a universe of ambiguity, this kind of certainty comes only once, and never again, no matter how many lifetimes you live.'

Richard took the truck across the intersection heading north. She looked for an instant past his face toward Harry's red taillights moving off into the fog and rain. The old Chevy pickup looked small beside a huge semitrailer rig roaring into Winterset, spraying a wave of road water over the last cowboy.

'Good-bye, Robert Kincaid,' she whispered, and began to cry, openly.

Richard looked over at her. 'What's wrong, Frannie? Will you *please* tell me what's wrong with you?'

'Richard, I just need some time to myself. I'll be all right in a few minutes.'

Richard tuned in the noon livestock reports, looked over at her, and shook his head.

Ashes

Night had come to Madison County. It was 1987, her sixty-seventh birthday. Francesca had been lying on her bed for two hours. She could see and touch and smell and hear all of it from twenty-two years ago.

She had remembered, then remembered again. The image of those red taillights moving west along Iowa 92 in the rain and fog had stalked her for more than two decades. She touched her breasts and could feel his chest muscles sweeping over them. God, she loved him so. Loved him then, more than she thought possible, loved him now even more. She would have done anything for him except destroy her family and maybe him as well.

She went down the stairs and sat at the old kitchen table with the yellow Formica top. Richard had bought a new one; he'd insisted on it. But she'd also asked that the old one be stored in a shed, and she had wrapped it carefully in plastic before it was put away.

'I don't see why you're so attached to this old table, anyway,' he had complained while helping her move it.

After Richard died, Michael had brought it back into the house for her and never asked why she wanted it in place of the newer one. He'd just looked at her in a questioning way. She'd said nothing.

Now she sat at the table. Then, going to the cupboard, she took down two white candles with small brass holders. She lit the candles and turned on the radio, slowly adjusting the dial until she found some quiet music.

She stood by the sink for a long time, her head tilted slightly upward, looking at his face, and whispered, 'I remember you, Robert Kincaid. Maybe the High-Desert Master was right. Maybe you were the last one. Maybe the cowboys *are* all close to dying by now.'

Before Richard died, she had never tried to call Kincaid or to write, either, though she had balanced on the knife edge of it every day for years. If she talked to him one more time, she would go to him. If she wrote him, she knew he would come for her. That's how close it was. Through the years he never called or wrote again, after sending her the one package with the photographs and the manuscript. She knew he understood how she felt and the complications he could cause in her life.

She subscribed to *National Geographic* in September of 1965. The article on the covered bridges appeared the following year, and there was Roseman Bridge in warm first light, the morning he had found her note. The cover was his photo of a team pulling a wagon toward Hogback Bridge. He had written the text for the article as well.

On the back page of the magazine, the writers and photographers were featured, and occasionally there were photographs of them. He was there sometimes. The same long silver hair, the bracelet, jeans or khakis, cameras hanging off his shoulders, the veins standing out on his arms. In the Kalahari, at the walls of Jaipur in India, in a canoe in Guatemala, in northern Canada. The road and the cowboy.

She clipped these and kept them in the manila envelope with the covered-bridge issue of the magazine, the manuscript, the two photographs, and his letter. She put the envelope beneath her underwear in the bureau, a place Richard would never look. And like some distant observer tracking him through the years, she watched Robert Kincaid grow older.

The grin was still there, even the long, lean body with the good muscles. But she could tell by the lines around his eyes, the slight droop of the strong shoulders, the slowly sagging face. She could tell. She had studied that body more closely than anything else in her life, more closely than her own body. And his ageing made her long even more for him, if that was possible. She suspected—no, she knew—he was by himself. And he was.

In the candlelight, at the table, she studied the clippings. He looked out at her from places far away. She came to the special picture from a 1967 issue. He was by a river in East Africa, facing the camera and up close to it, squatting down, getting ready to take a photograph of something.

When she had first looked at this clipping, years ago, she could see the silver chain around his neck now had a small medallion attached to it. Michael was away at college, and when Richard and Carolyn had gone to bed, she got out a powerful magnifying glass Michael had used for his stamp collection when he was young and brought it close to the photo.

'My God,' she breathed. The medallion said 'Francesca' on it. That was his one small indiscretion, and she forgave him for it, smiling. In all of the photos after that, the medallion was always there on the silver chain.

After 1975 she never saw him again in the magazine. His byline was absent as well. She searched every issue but found nothing. He would have been sixty-two that year.

When Richard died in 1979, when the funeral was over and the children had gone back to their own homes, she thought about calling Robert Kincaid. He would be sixty-six; she was fifty-nine. There was still time, even with the loss of fourteen years. She thought hard about it for a week and finally took the number off his letterhead and dialled it.

Her heart nearly stopped when the phone began to

ring. She heard the receiver being picked up and almost put the phone back on the hook. A woman's voice said, 'McGregor Insurance.' Francesca sank but recovered enough to ask the secretary if she had dialled the correct number. She had. Francesca thanked her and hung up.

Next she tried the Information operator in Bellingham, Washington. Nothing listed. She tried Seattle. Nothing. Then the Chamber of Commerce offices in Bellingham and Seattle. She asked if they would check the city directories. They did, and he was not listed. He could be anywhere, she thought.

She remembered the magazine; he had said to call there. The receptionist was polite but new, and had to get someone to help her with the request. Francesca's call was transferred three times before she talked with an associate editor who had been at the magazine for twenty years. She asked about Robert Kincaid.

Of course the editor remembered him. 'Trying to locate him, huh? He was a hell of a photographer, if you'll excuse the language. He was cantankerous, not in a nasty way, but persistent. He was after art for art's sake, and that doesn't work very well with our readership. Our readership wants nice pictures, skilful pictures, but nothing too wild.

'We always said Kincaid was a little strange; none of us knew him well outside of the work he did for us. But he was a pro. We could send him anywhere, and he'd deliver, even though he disagreed with our editorial

147

decisions most of the time. As for his whereabouts, I've been checking our files while we talked. He left the magazine in 1975. The address and phone number I have are ...' He read off the same information Francesca already had. She stopped trying after that, mostly because she was afraid of what she might discover.

She drifted along, allowing herself to think more and more about Robert Kincaid. She was still able to drive well enough, and several times a year she would go to Des Moines and have lunch in the restaurant where he had taken her. On one of those trips, she bought a leather-bound book of blank pages. And on those pages she began recording in neat handwriting the details of her love affair with him and her thoughts about him. It required nearly three volumes of the notebooks before she was satisfied she had completed her task.

Winterset was improving. There was an active art guild, mostly female, and talk of refurbishing the old bridges had been going on for some years. Interesting young folks were building houses in the hills. Things had loosened up, long hair was no longer cause for stares, though sandals on men were still pretty scarce and poets were few.

Yet except for a few women friends, she withdrew completely from the community. People remarked about it and how they often would see her standing by Roseman Bridge and sometimes by Cedar Bridge. Old folks frequently become strange, they said, and contented themselves with that explanation.

On the second of February 1982, a United Parcel Service truck trundled up her driveway. She hadn't ordered anything she could recall. Puzzled, she signed for the package and looked at the address: 'Francesca Johnson, RR 2, Winterset, Iowa 50273.' The return address was a law firm in Seattle.

The package was neatly wrapped and carried extra insurance. She placed it on the kitchen table and opened it carefully. Inside were three boxes, packed securely in Styrofoam peanuts. Taped to the top of one was a small padded envelope. To another was taped a business envelope addressed to her and carrying the law firm's return address.

She removed the tape from the business envelope and opened it, shaking.

January 25, 1982

Ms Francesca Johnson
RR 2
Winterset, IA 50273

Dear Ms Johnson:

We represent the estate of one Robert L Kincaid,
who recently passed away ...

Francesca laid the letter on the table. Outside, snow

blew across the fields of winter. She watched it skim the stubble, taking corn husks with it, piling them up in the corner of the wire. She read the words once more.

We represent the estate of one Robert L. Kincaid,
who recently passed away. . . .

'Oh, Robert . . . Robert . . . no.' She said it softly and bowed her head.

An hour later she was able to continue reading. The straightforward language of the law, the precision of the words, angered her.

'We represent . . .'

An attorney carrying out his duties to a client.

But the power, the leopard who came riding in on the tail of a comet, the shaman who was looking for Roseman Bridge on a hot August day, and the man who stood on the running board of a truck named Harry and looked back at her dying in the dust of an Iowa farm lane—where was he in those words?

The letter should have been a thousand pages long. It should have talked about the end of evolutionary chains and the loss of free range, about cowboys struggling with the corners of the wire, like the corn husks of winter.

The only will he left was dated July 8, 1967.

His instructions about having the enclosed items delivered to you were explicit. If you could not be found, the materials were to be incinerated.

Also enclosed inside the box marked with the word 'Letter' is a message for you he left with us in 1978. He sealed the envelope, and it has been left unopened.

Mr Kincaid's remains were cremated. At his request, no marker was placed anywhere. His ashes were scattered, also at his request, near your home by an associate of ours. I believe the location was called Roseman Bridge.

If we may be of further service, please do not hesitate to contact us.

Sincerely yours,
Allen B. Quippen, Attorney at Law

She caught her breath, dried her eyes again, and began to examine the remaining contents of the box.

She knew what was in the small padded envelope. She knew it as surely as she knew spring would come again this year. She opened it carefully and reached in. Out came the silver chain. The medallion attached to it was scratched and read 'Francesca.' On the back, etched in the tiniest of letters, was: 'If found, please send to Francesca Johnson, RR 2, Winterset, Iowa, USA.'

His silver bracelet was wrapped in tissue paper at the bottom of the envelope. A slip of paper was included with the bracelet. It was her handwriting:

*If you'd like supper again when 'white moths are on the wing,'
come by tonight after you're finished.*

Her note from the Roseman Bridge. He'd kept even that for his memories.

Then she remembered that was the only thing he had of hers, his only evidence she existed, aside from elusive images on slowly decaying film emulsions. The little note from Roseman Bridge. It was stained and curved, as if it had been carried in a billfold for a long time.

She wondered how many times he had read it over the years, far from the hills along Middle River. She could imagine him holding the note before him in the thin light of a reading lamp on a nonstop jet to somewhere, sitting on the floor of a bamboo hut in tiger country and reading it by flashlight, folding and putting it away on a rainy night in Bellingham, then looking at photographs of a woman leaning against a fence post on a summer morning or coming out of a covered bridge at sundown.

The three boxes each contained a camera with a lens attached. They were battered, scarred. Turning one around, she could read 'Nikon' on the viewfinder and, just to the upper left of the Nikon label, the letter *F*. It was the camera she had handed him at Cedar Bridge.

Finally she opened the letter from him. It was written

in longhand on his stationery and dated August 16, 1978.

Dear Francesca,

I hope this finds you well. I don't know when you'll receive it. Sometime after I'm gone. I'm sixty-five now, and it's been thirteen years ago today that we met when I came up your lane looking for directions.

I'm gambling that this package won't upset your life in any way. I just couldn't bear to think of the cameras sitting in a secondhand case in a camera store or in some stranger's hands. They'll be in pretty rough shape by the time you get them. But, I have no one else to leave them to, and I apologize for putting you at risk by sending them to you.

I was on the road almost constantly from 1965 to 1975. Just to remove some of the temptation to call you or come for you, a temptation I have virtually every waking moment of my life, I took all of the overseas assignments I could find. There have been times, many of them, when I've said, 'The hell with it. I'm going to Winterset, Iowa, and, whatever the cost, take Francesca away with me.'

But I remember your words, and I respect your feelings. Maybe you were right; I just don't know. I do know that driving out of your lane that hot Friday morning was the hardest thing I've ever done or will ever do. In fact, I doubt if few men have ever done anything more difficult than that.

I left National Geographic *in 1975 and have been devoting the remainder of my shooting years mostly to things of my own choosing, picking up a little work where I can get it, local or regional stuff that keeps me away only a few days at a time. It's been tough financially, but I get along. I always do.*

Much of my work is around Puget Sound. I like it that way. It seems as men get older they turn toward the water.

Oh, yes, I have a dog now, a golden retriever. I call him 'Highway,' and he travels with me most of the time, head hanging out the window, looking for good shots.

In 1972, I fell down a cliff in Maine, in Acadia National Park, and broke my ankle.

The chain and medallion got torn off in the fall. Fortunately they landed close by. I found them again, and a jeweller mended the chain.

I live with dust on my heart. That's about as well as I can put it. There were women before you, a few, but none after. I made no conscious pledge to celibacy; I'm just not interested.

I once watched a Canada goose whose mate had been shot by hunters. They mate for life, you know. The gander circled the pond for days, and more days after that. When I last saw him, he was swimming alone through the wild rice, still looking. I suppose that analogy is a little too obvious for literary tastes, but it's pretty much the way I feel.

In my imagination, on foggy mornings or afternoons with the sun bouncing off northwest water, I try to think of where you might be in your life and what you might be doing as I'm thinking of you. Nothing complicated—going out to your garden, sitting on your front porch swing, standing at the sink in your kitchen. Things like that.

I remember everything. How you smelled, how you tasted like the summer. The feel of your skin against mine, and the sound of your whispers as I loved you.

Robert Penn Warren once used the phrase 'a world that seems to be God-abandoned.' Not bad, pretty close to how I feel some of the time. But I cannot live that way always. When those feelings become too strong, I load Harry and go down the road with Highway for a few days.

I don't like feeling sorry for myself. That's not who I am. And most of the time I don't feel that way. Instead, I am grateful for having at least found you. We could have flashed by one another like two pieces of cosmic dust.

God or the universe or whatever one chooses to label the great systems of balance and order does not recognize Earth-time. To the universe, four days is no different than four billion light years. I try to keep that in mind.

But, I am, after all, a man. And all the philosophic rationalizations I can conjure up do not keep me from wanting you, every day, every moment, the merciless wail of time, of time I can never spend with you, deep within my head.

I love you, profoundly and completely. And I always will.

The last cowboy,
Robert

P.S., I put another new engine in Harry last summer, and he's doing fine.

The package arrived five years ago. And looking at the contents had become part of her annual birthday ritual. She kept his cameras, bracelet, and the chain with the medallion in a special chest in the closet. A local carpenter had made the box to her design, out of walnut, with dust seals and padded interior sections. 'Pretty fancy box,' he had said. Francesca had only smiled.

The last part of the ritual was the manuscript. She always read it by candlelight, at the end of the day. She brought it from the living room and laid it carefully on the yellow Formica, near a candle, lit her one cigarette of the year, a Camel, took a sip of brandy, and began to read.

Falling from Dimension Z

ROBERT KINCAID

There are old winds I still do not understand, though I have been riding, forever it seems, along the curl of their spines. I move in Dimension Z; the world goes by somewhere else in another slice of things, parallel to me. As if, hands in my pockets and bending a little forward, I see it through a department store window, looking inward.

In Dimension Z, there are strange moments. Coming around a long, rainy, New Mexico curve west of Magdalena, the highway turns to a footpath and the path to an animal trail. A pass of my wiper blades, and the trail becomes a forest place where nothing has ever gone. Again the wiper blades and, again, something further back. Great ice, this time. I am moving through short grass, in furs, with matted hair and spear, thin and hard as the ice itself, all muscle and implacable cunning. Past the ice, still further back along the measure of things, deep salt water in which I swim, gilled and scaled. I cannot see more than that, except beyond plankton is the digit zero.

Euclid was not always right. He assumed parallelness, in constancy, right to the end of things; but a non-Euclidean way of being is also possible, where the lines come together, far out there. A vanishing point. The illusion of convergence.

Yet I know it's more than illusion. Sometimes a coming together is possible, a spilling of one reality into another. A kind of soft enlacing. Not prim intersections loomed in a world of precision, no sound of the shuttle. Just ... well ... breathing. Yes, that's the sound of it, maybe the feel of it, too. Breathing.

And I move slowly over this other reality, and beside it and underneath and around it, always with strength, always with power, yet always with a giving of myself to it. And the other senses this, coming forward with its own power, giving itself to me, in turn.

Somewhere, inside of the breathing, music sounds, and the curious spiral dance begins then, with a metre all its own that tempers the ice-man with spear and matted hair. And slowly—rolling and turning in adagio, in adagio always—ice-man falls ... from Dimension Z ... and into her.

At the end of her sixty-seventh birthday, when the rain had stopped, Francesca put the manila envelope in the bottom drawer of the rolltop desk. She had decided to keep it in her safe deposit box at the bank after Richard died but brought it home for a few days each year at this time. The lid on the walnut chest was shut on the cameras, and the chest was placed on the closet shelf in her bedroom.

Earlier in the afternoon, she had visited Roseman Bridge. Now she walked out on the porch, dried off the swing with a towel, and sat down. It was cold, but she would stay for a few minutes, as she always did. Then she walked to the yard gate and stood. Then to the head of the lane. Twenty-two years later, she could see him stepping from his truck in the late afternoon, trying to find his way; she could see Harry bouncing toward the county road, then stopping, and Robert Kincaid standing on the running board, looking back up the lane.

A Letter from Francesca

FRANCESCA JOHNSON DIED in January of 1989. She was sixty-nine years old at the time of her death. Robert Kincaid would have been seventy-six that year. The cause of death was listed as 'natural.' 'She just died,' the doctor told Michael and Carolyn. 'Actually, we're a little perplexed. We can find no specific cause for her death. A neighbour found her slumped over the kitchen table.'

In a 1982 letter to her attorney, she had requested that her remains be cremated and her ashes scattered at Roseman Bridge. Cremation was an uncommon practice in Madison County—viewed as slightly radical in some undefined way—and her wish generated considerable discussion at the cafe, the Texaco station, and the implement dealership. The disposition of her ashes was not made public.

Following the memorial service, Michael and Carolyn drove slowly to Roseman Bridge and carried out Francesca's instructions. Though it was nearby, the bridge had never been special to the Johnson family, and they wondered, and wondered again, why their rather sensible mother would behave in such an enigmatic way and why she had not asked to be buried by their father, as was customary.

Following that, Michael and Carolyn began the long process of sorting through the house and brought home the materials from the safe deposit box after they were examined by the local attorney for estate purposes and released.

They divided the materials from the box and began looking through them. The manila envelope was in Carolyn's stack, about a third of the way down. She was puzzled when she opened it and removed the contents. She read Robert Kincaid's 1965 letter to Francesca. After that she read his 1978 letter, then the 1982 letter from the Seattle attorney. Finally she studied the magazine clippings.

'Michael.'

He caught the mixture of surprise and pensiveness in her voice and looked up immediately. 'What is it?'

Carolyn had tears in her eyes, and her voice became unsteady. 'Mother was in love with a man named Robert Kincaid. He was a photographer. Remember when we all had to see the copy of *National Geographic* with the bridge story in it? He was the one who took the pictures of the bridges here. And remember all the kids talking about the strange-looking guy with the cameras back then? That was him.'

Michael sat across from her, his tie loosened, collar open. 'Say that again, slowly. I can't believe I heard you correctly.'

After reading the letters, Michael searched the downstairs closet, then went upstairs to Francesca's bedroom. He had never noticed the walnut box before and opened it. He carried it down to the kitchen table. 'Carolyn, here are his cameras.'

Tucked in one end of the box was a sealed envelope with 'Carolyn or Michael' written on it in Francesca's script, and lying between the cameras were three leather-bound notebooks.

'I'm not sure I'm capable of reading what's in that envelope,' said Michael. 'Read it out loud to me, if you can handle it.'

She opened the envelope and read aloud.

January 7, 1987

Dear Carolyn and Michael,

Though I'm feeling just fine, I think it's time for me to get my affairs in order (as they say). There is something, something very important, you need to know about. That's why I'm writing this.

After looking through the safe deposit box and finding the large manila envelope addressed to me with a 1965 postmark, I'm sure you'll eventually come to this letter. If possible, please sit at the old kitchen table to read it. You'll understand that request shortly.

It's hard for me to write this to my own children, but I must.

There's something here that's too strong, too beautiful, to die with me. And if you are to know who your mother was, all the goods and bads, you need to know what I'm about to say. Brace yourself.

As you've already discovered, his name was Robert Kincaid. His middle initial was 'L,' but I never knew what the L represented. He was a photographer, and he was here in 1965 photographing the covered bridges.

Remember how excited the town was when the pictures appeared in National Geographic You may also recall that I began receiving the magazine about that time. Now you know the reason for my sudden interest in it. By the way, I was with him (carrying one of his camera knapsacks) when the photo of Cedar Bridge was taken.

Understand, I loved your father in a quiet fashion. I knew it then, I know it now. He was good to me and gave me the two of you, who I treasure. Don't forget that.

But Robert Kincaid was something quite different, like nobody I've ever seen or heard or read about through my entire life. To make you understand him completely is impossible. First of all, you are not me. Second, you would have had to have been around him, to watch him move, to hear him talk about being on a dead-end branch of evolution. Maybe the notebooks and magazine clippings will help, but even those will not be enough.

In a way, he was not of this earth. That's about as clear as I can say it. I've always thought of him as a leopardlike creature who rode in on the tail of a comet. He moved that way, his body was like that. He somehow coupled enormous intensity with warmth and kindness, and there was a vague sense of tragedy about him. He felt he was becoming obsolete in a world of computers and robots and organized living in general. He saw

166

himself as one of the last cowboys, as he put it, and called himself old-fangled.

The first time I ever saw him was when he stopped and asked directions to Roseman Bridge. The three of you were at the Illinois State Fair. Believe me, I was not scouting around for any adventure. That was the furthest thing from my mind. But I looked at him for less than five seconds, and I knew I wanted him, though not as much as I eventually came to want him.

And please don't think of him as some Casanova running around taking advantage of country girls. He wasn't like that at all. In fact, he was a little shy, and I had as much to do with what happened as he did. More, in fact. The note tucked in with his bracelet is one I posted on Roseman Bridge so he would see it the morning after we first met. Aside from his photographs of me, it's the only piece of evidence he had over the years that I actually existed, that I was not just some dream he had.

I know children have a tendency to think of their parents as rather asexual, so I hope what I'm going to say won't shock you, and I certainly hope it won't destroy your memory of me.

In our old kitchen, Robert and I spent hours together. We talked and danced by candlelight. And, yes, we made love there and in the bedroom and in the pasture grass and just about anywhere else you can think of. It was incredible, powerful, transcending lovemaking, and it went on for days, almost without stopping. I always have used the word 'powerful' a lot in thinking about him. For that's what he had become by the time we met.

He was like an arrow in his intensity. I simply was helpless when he made love to me. Not weak; that's not what I felt. Just, well, overwhelmed by his sheer emotional and physical power.

167

Once when I whispered that to him, he simply said, 'I am the highway and a peregrine and all the sails that ever went to sea.'

I checked the dictionary later. The first thing people think of when they hear the word 'peregrine' is a falcon. But there are other meanings of the word, and he would have been aware of that. One is 'foreigner, alien.' A second is 'roving or wandering, migratory.' The Latin peregrinus, which is one root of the word, means a stranger. He was all of those things—a stranger, a foreigner in the more general sense of the word, a wanderer, and he also was falconlike, now that I think of it.

Children, understand I am trying to express what cannot be put into words. I only wish that someday you each might have what I experienced; however, I'm beginning to think that's not likely. Though I suppose it's not fashionable to say such things in these more enlightened times, I don't think it's possible for a woman to possess the peculiar kind of power Robert Kincaid had. So, Michael, that lets you out. As for Carolyn, I'm afraid the bad news is that there was only one of him, and no more.

If not for your father and the two of you, I would have gone anywhere with him, instantly. He asked me to go, begged me to go. But I wouldn't, and he was too much of a sensitive and caring person to ever interfere in our lives after that.

The paradox is this: If it hadn't been for Robert Kincaid, I'm not sure I could have stayed on the farm all these years. In four days, he gave me a lifetime, a universe, and made the separate parts of me into a whole. I have never stopped thinking of him, not for a moment. Even when he was not in my conscious mind, I could feel him somewhere, always he was there.

But it never took away from anything I felt for the two of you or your father. Thinking only of myself for a moment, I'm not sure I made the right decision. But taking the family into account, I'm pretty sure I did.

Though I must be honest and tell you that, right from the outset, Robert understood better than I what it was the two of us formed with each other. I think I only began to grasp its significance over time, gradually. Had I truly understood that, when he was face to face with me and asking me to go, I probably would have left with him.

Robert believed the world had become too rational, had stopped trusting in magic as much as it should. I've often wondered if I was too rational in making my decision.

I'm sure you found my burial request incomprehensible, thinking perhaps it was the product of a confused old woman. After reading the 1982 Seattle attorney's letter and my notebooks, you'll understand why I made that request. I gave my family my life; I gave Robert Kincaid what was left of me.

I think Richard knew there was something in me he could not reach, and I sometimes wonder if he found the manila envelope when I kept it at home in the bureau. Just before he died, I was sitting by him in a Des Moines hospital, and he said this to me: 'Francesca, I know you had your own dreams, too. I'm sorry I couldn't give them to you.' That was the most touching moment of our lives together.

I don't want to make you feel guilt or pity or any of those things. That's not my purpose here. I only want you to know how much I loved Robert Kincaid. I dealt with it day by day, all these years, just as he did.

Though we never spoke again to one another, we remained bound together as tightly as it's possible for two people to be bound. I cannot find the words to express this adequately. He said it best when he told me we had ceased being separate beings and, instead, had become a third being formed by the two of us. Neither of us existed independent of that being. And that being was left to wander.

Carolyn, remember the horrible argument we had once about the light pink dress in my closet? You had seen it and wanted to wear it. You said you never remembered me wearing it, so why couldn't it be made over to fit you. That was the dress I wore the first night Robert and I made love. I've never looked as good in my entire life as I did that night. The dress was my small and foolish memory of that time. That's why I never wore it again and why I refused to let you wear it.

After Robert left here in 1965, I realized I knew very little about him, in terms of his family history. Though I think I learned almost everything else about him—everything that really counted—in those few short days. He was an only child, both his parents were dead, and he was born in a small town in Ohio.

I'm not even sure if he went to college or even high school, but he had an intelligence that was brilliant in a raw, primitive, almost mystical fashion. Oh yes, he was a combat photographer with the Marines in the South Pacific during World War II.

He was married once and divorced, a long time before he met me. There were no children. His wife had been a musician of some kind, a folksinger I think he said, and his long absences on photographic expeditions were just too hard on the marriage. He took the blame for the breakup.

Other than that, Robert had no family, as far as I know. I am asking you to make him part of ours, however difficult that may seem to you at first. At least I had a family, a life with others. Robert was alone. That was not fair, and I knew it.

I prefer, at least I think I do, because of Richard's memory and the way people talk, that all of this be kept within the Johnson family, somehow. I'll leave it to your judgment, though.

In any case, I'm certainly not ashamed of what Robert Kincaid and I had together. On the contrary. I loved him desperately throughout all these years, though, for my own reasons, I tried to contact him only once. That was after your father died. The attempt failed, and I was afraid something had happened to him, so I never tried again out of that fear. I simply couldn't face that reality. So you can imagine how I felt when the package with the attorney's letter arrived in 1982.

As I said, I hope you understand and don't think ill of me. If you love me, then you must love what I have done.

Robert Kincaid taught me what it was like to be a woman in a way that few women, maybe none, will ever experience. He was fine and warm, and he deserves, certainly, your respect and maybe your love. I hope you can give him both of those. In his own way, through me, he was good to you.

Go well, my children.
Mother

There was silence in the old kitchen. Michael took a deep breath and looked out the window. Carolyn looked around her, at the sink, the floor, at the table, at everything.

When she spoke, her voice was almost a whisper. 'Oh, Michael, Michael, think of them all those years, wanting each other so desperately. She gave him up for us and for Dad. And Robert Kincaid stayed away out of respect for her feelings about us. Michael, I can hardly deal with the thought of it. We treat our marriages so casually, and we were part of the reason that an incredible love affair ended the way it did.

'They had four days together, just four. Out of a lifetime. It was when we went to that ridiculous state fair in Illinois. Look at the picture of Mom. I never saw her like that. She's so beautiful, and it's not the photograph. It's what he did for her. Just look at her; she's wild and free. Her hair's blowing in the wind, her face is alive. She just looks wonderful.'

'Jesus,' was all Michael could say, wiping his forehead with the kitchen towel and dabbing at his eyes when Carolyn wasn't looking.

Carolyn spoke again. 'Apparently he never tried to contact her all these years. And he must have died alone; that's why he had the cameras sent to her.

'I remember the fight Mom and I had over the pink dress. It went on for days. I whined and asked why. Then I refused to speak to her. All she ever said was, "No, Carolyn, not that one."'

And Michael remembered the old table at which they were sitting. That's why Francesca had asked him to bring it back into the kitchen after their father died.

Carolyn opened the small padded envelope. 'Here's his bracelet and his silver chain and medallion. And here's the note Mother mentioned in her letter, the one she put on Roseman Bridge. That's why the photo he sent of the bridge shows the piece of paper tacked to it.

'Michael, what are we going to do? Think about it for a moment; I'll be right back.'

She ran up the stairs and returned in a few minutes carrying the pink dress folded carefully in plastic. She shook it out and held it up for Michael to see.

'Just imagine her wearing this and dancing with him here in the kitchen. Think of all the time we've spent here and the images she must have seen while cooking and sitting here with us, talking about our problems, about where to go to college, about how hard it is to have a successful marriage. God, we're so innocent and immature compared to her.'

Michael nodded and turned to the cupboards above the sink. 'Do you suppose Mother kept anything to drink around here? Lord knows I can use it. And, to answer your question, I don't know what we're going to do.'

He rummaged through the cupboards and found a bottle of brandy, almost empty. 'There's enough for two drinks here, Carolyn. Want one?'

'Yes.'

Michael took the only two brandy glasses from the cupboard and set them on the yellow Formica table. He emptied Francesca's last bottle of brandy into them, while Carolyn silently began reading volume one of the notebooks. 'Robert Kincaid came to me on the sixteenth of August, a Monday, in 1965. He was trying to find Roseman Bridge. It was late afternoon, hot, and he was driving a pickup truck he called Harry. . . .'

Postscript:
The Tacoma Nighthawk

As I wrote the story of Robert Kincaid and Francesca Johnson, I became more and more intrigued with Kincaid and how little any of us knew about him and his life. Only a few weeks before the book went to the printer's, I flew to Seattle and tried again to uncover additional information about him.

I had an idea that since he liked music, and was an artist himself, there might have been someone in the music and art culture of the Puget Sound area who knew him. The arts editor of the *Seattle Times* was helpful. Though he did not know of Kincaid, he provided me access to pertinent sections of the newspaper from 1975 through 1982, the period in which I was most interested.

Working through the 1980 editions, I came across a photo of a black jazz musician, a tenor saxophone player named John 'Nighthawk' Cummings. And beside the photo was the credit line *Robert Kincaid*. The local musician's union provided me with Cummings's address, advising me that he had not played actively for some years. The address was on a side street near an industrial section of Tacoma, just off Highway 5 running down from Seattle.

It took several visits to his apartment before I found him at home. He was wary, initially, of my inquiries. But I convinced him I had a serious and benign interest in Kincaid, and he became cordial and open after that. What follows is a slightly edited transcript of my interview with Cummings, who was seventy at the time I talked with him. I simply turned on my tape recorder and let him tell me about Robert Kincaid.

Interview with 'Nighthawk' Cummings

I WAS DOIN' a gig at Shorty's, up in Seattle where I was livin' at the time, and I needed a good black-and-white glossy of myself for publicity. The bass player told me there was a guy livin' out on one of the islands who did some good work. He didn't have a phone, so I sent him a postcard.

He came by, a real strange-lookin' old dude in jeans and boots and orange suspenders, takes out these old beat-up cameras that didn't even look like they'd work, and I thought, Uh-oh. He put me up against a light-coloured wall with my horn and told me to play and keep on playing. So I played. For the first three minutes or so, the guy just stood there and looked at me hard, real hard, with the coolest blue eyes you've ever seen.

After a little while, he starts takin' pictures. Then he asks if I'll play 'Autumn Leaves.' And I do that. I play the tune for maybe ten minutes straight while he keeps banging away with his cameras, takin' one shot after another. Then he says, 'Fine, I've got it. I'll have them for you tomorrow.'

181

Next day he brings them by, and I'm knocked over. I've had a lot of pictures taken of me, but these were the best, by far. He charged me fifty dollars, which seemed pretty cheap to me. He thanks me, leaves, and on his way out asks where I'm playin'. So I tell him, 'Shorty's.'

A few nights later, I look out at the audience and see him sittin' at a table off in the corner, listenin' real hard. Well, he started comin' in once a week, always on a Tuesday, always drank beer, but not much of it.

I sometimes went over on breaks and talked with him for a few minutes. He was quiet, didn't say a lot, but real pleasant, always asked politely if I'd mind playin' 'Autumn Leaves.'

After a while we got to know each other a little. I used to like to go down to the harbour and watch the water and ships; turns out, so did he. So we got to the point we'd sit on a bench for whole afternoons and talk. Just a couple of old guys winding it down, starting to feel a little irrelevant, a little obsolete.

Used to bring his dog along. Nice dog. Called him Highway.

He understood magic. Jazz musicians understand it, too. That's probably why we got along. You're playing some tune you've played a thousand times before, and suddenly there's a whole new set of ideas coming straight out of your horn without ever going through your conscious mind. He said photography and life in general

182

were a lot like that. Then he added, 'So is making love to a woman you love.'

He was workin' on somethin' where he was tryin' to convert music into visual images. He said to me, 'John, you know that riff you almost always play in the fourth measure of "Sophisticated Lady"? Well, I think I got that on film the other morning. The light came across the water just right and a blue heron kind of looped through my viewfinder all at the same time. I could actually *see* your riff while I was hearing it and hit the shutter.'

He spent all his time on this music-into-images thing. Was obsessed by it. Don't know how he made a living.

He never said much about his own life. I knew he'd travelled a lot doing photography, but not much more until one day I asked him about the little silver thing he had on a chain around his neck. Up close, I could see the name *Francesca* on it. So I asked him, 'Anything special about that?'

He didn't say anything for a while, just stared out at the water. Then he said, 'How much time do you have?' Well, it was a Monday, my night off, so I told him I had as much as it took.

He started talkin'. It was like a faucet got turned on. Talked all afternoon and most of the night. I had the feelin' he'd kept this all inside of him for a long time.

Never mentioned the woman's last name, never said where it all took place. But, man, this Robert Kincaid was a poet when he talked about her. She must've really been something, one incredible lady. Started quotin' from a piece he'd written for her—something about Dimension Z, as I recall. I remember thinking it sounded like one of Ornette Coleman's free-form improvisations.

And, man, he cried while he talked. He cried *big* tears, the kind it takes an old man to cry, the kind it takes a saxophone to play. Afterward, I understood why he always requested 'Autumn Leaves.' And, man, I started to love this guy. Anyone who can feel that way about a woman is worth lovin' himself.

So I got to thinkin' about it, about the power of this thing he and the woman had. About what he called the 'old ways.' And I said to myself, 'I've got to play that power, that love affair, make those old ways come out of my horn.' There was somethin' so damn lyrical about it.

So I wrote this tune—took me three months. I wanted to keep it simple, elegant. Complex things are easy to do. Simplicity's the real challenge. I worked on it every day until I began to get it right. Then I worked on it some more and wrote out some lead sheets for the piano and bass. Finally, one night I played it.

He was out there in the audience; Tuesday night, as usual. Anyway, it's a slow night, maybe twenty people in the place, nobody payin' much attention to the group.

He's sittin' there, quietly, listenin' hard like he always

did, and I say over the microphone, 'I'm gonna play a tune I wrote for a friend of mine. It's called "Francesca."'

I watched him when I said it. He's starin' at his bottle of beer, but when I said 'Francesca,' he slowly looked up at me, brushed back his long grey hair with both hands, lit a Camel, and those blue eyes came right at me.

I made that horn sound like it never had before; I made it cry for all the miles and years that separated them. There was a little melodic figure in the first measure that sort of pronounced her name—'Fran ... ces ... ca.'

When I finished, he stood real straight by his table, smiled and nodded, paid his bill, and left. After that I always played it when he came by. He framed a photograph of an old covered bridge and gave it to me for writin' the song. It's hangin' right over there. Never told me where he took it, but it says 'Roseman Bridge' right below his signature.

One Tuesday night, seven, maybe eight years ago, he doesn't show. He's not there the next week, either. I think maybe he's sick or somethin'. I start to worry, go down to the harbour, ask around. Nobody knows nothin' about him. Finally, I take a boat over to the island where he lived. It was an old cabin—shack, really—down by the water.

While I'm pokin' around, a neighbour comes over

and asks what I'm doin'. So I tell him. Neighbour says he died about ten days ago. Man, I hurt when I heard that. Still do. I liked that guy a lot. There was somethin' about that cat, somethin'. I had the feelin' there were things he knew that the rest of us don't.

I asked this neighbour about the dog. He doesn't know. Said he didn't know Kincaid, either. So I call the pound, and sure enough they've got old Highway down there. I go down and get him out and gave him to my nephew. The last I saw of him, he and the kid were having a love affair. I felt good about that.

Anyway, that's about it. Not long after I found out what happened to Kincaid, my left arm started going numb when I play for more than twenty minutes. Something to do with a vertebra problem. So I don't work anymore.

But, man, I'm haunted by that story he told me about him and the woman. So, every Tuesday night I get out my horn, and I play that tune I wrote for him. I play it here, all by myself.

And for some reason I always look at that picture he gave me while I play it. Somethin' about it, don't know what it is, but I can't take my eyes off that picture when I play the tune.

I just stand here, 'bout twilight, makin' that ol' horn weep, and I play that tune for a man named Robert Kincaid and a woman he called Francesca.